Savage Vow

BLUEBLOOD VAMPIRES BOOK FOUR

MICHELLE HERCULES

INFINITE SKU PUBLISHING

Cover Illustration: Jemlin

ISBN: 978-1-959167-07-5

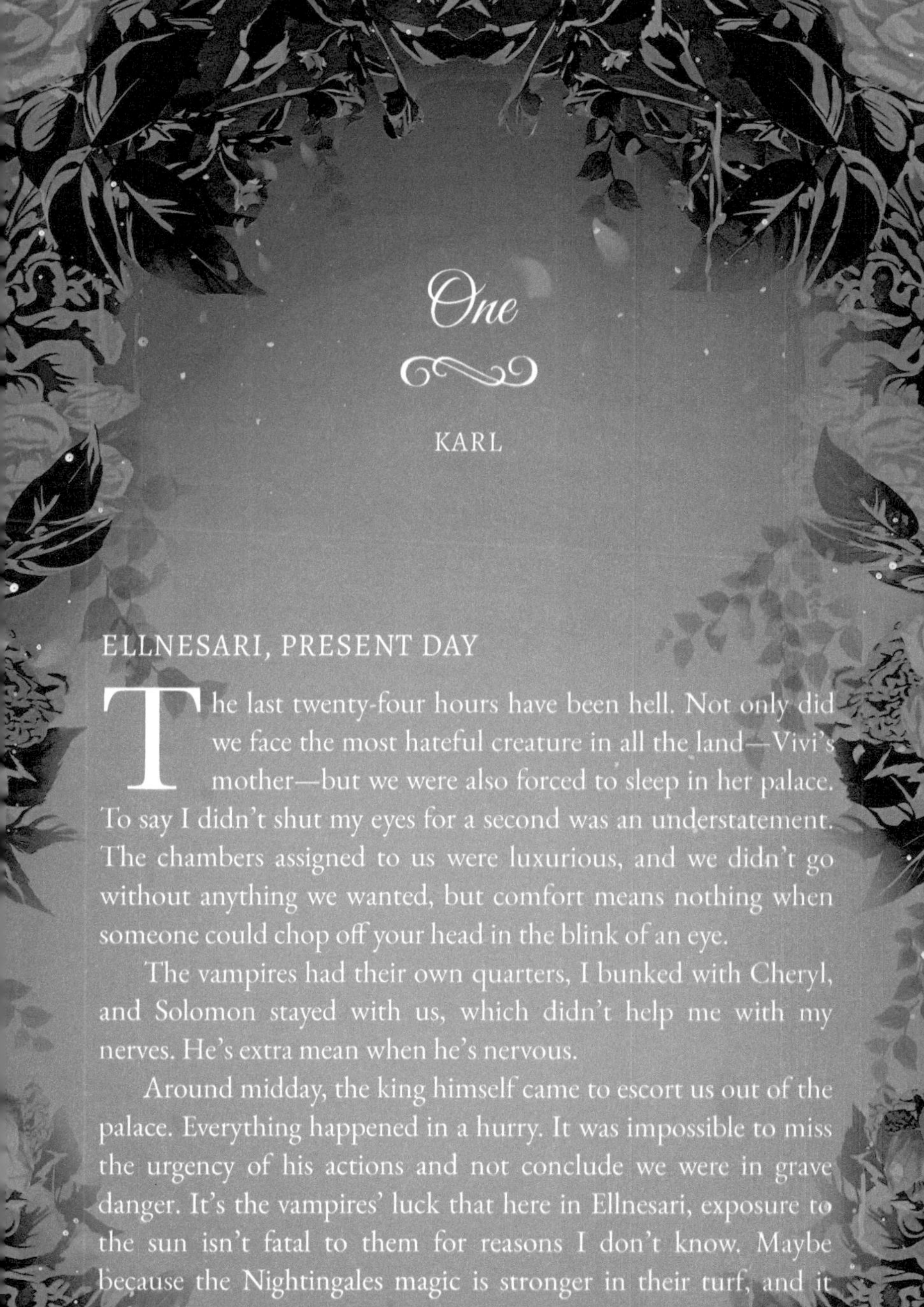

One

KARL

ELLNESARI, PRESENT DAY

The last twenty-four hours have been hell. Not only did we face the most hateful creature in all the land—Vivi's mother—but we were also forced to sleep in her palace. To say I didn't shut my eyes for a second was an understatement. The chambers assigned to us were luxurious, and we didn't go without anything we wanted, but comfort means nothing when someone could chop off your head in the blink of an eye.

The vampires had their own quarters, I bunked with Cheryl, and Solomon stayed with us, which didn't help me with my nerves. He's extra mean when he's nervous.

Around midday, the king himself came to escort us out of the palace. Everything happened in a hurry. It was impossible to miss the urgency of his actions and not conclude we were in grave danger. It's the vampires' luck that here in Ellnesari, exposure to the sun isn't fatal to them for reasons I don't know. Maybe because the Nightingales magic is stronger in their turf, and it offers the vampires protection.

He told us to wear a special cloak and warned us to not remove it under any circumstances. Then he dumped us in the middle of a peculiar-looking part of the forest he called Hornet's Gardens.

Aurora has been pacing since the king left us here, frantic with worry about her sister, who spent the night with Rikkon.

"Will you quit trying to dig a hole in the ground, girl?" Solomon pipes up.

She whirls around and levels the small male with a glare. "I'm sorry. Is my worrying for my sister's life getting on your nerves?"

He glowers. "As a matter of fact, yes. She's the safest out of all of us. Rikkon won't let any harm come to her."

"That doesn't comfort me," she retorts. "Not when his mother made it clear she doesn't approve of their relationship."

Saxon tosses his arm over her shoulders and pulls her closer. "It's going to be okay, Rora."

There's a visible change in the witch. She melts into her mate's embrace, and the sight makes me uneasy. Once upon a time, I thought I had found someone who reacted the same way from my touch, but it turned out to be a cruel fantasy.

Automatically, I glance in Manu's direction, feeling the sting of betrayal still as sharp as when it was delivered.

Cheryl steps next to me and whispers, "Have you noticed how quiet Manu has been this whole time?"

There's no lost love between my sister and Manu, so the fact that she's noticing something about Manu proves her behavior is indeed quite strange. I've been trying my best to ignore her. Being forced to resume my duties as her familiar is torture, but King Raphael was insistent that I put my issues aside for the greater good. I couldn't say no to him, even if he didn't have solid reasoning for his request. He spared my sister's life when she was turned, and that is a debt I'll never be able to repay.

The air ripples with magic, putting me and all the others on high alert. A second later, Rikkon and Miranda materialize out of thin air. Aurora rushes to her sister, yanking her from Rikkon's side to engulf her in a tight hug.

"Are you okay?" Aurora asks. "I barely had a chance to talk to you yesterday."

"I'm fine, Rora."

Vivi steps forward, her attention on her brother. "Rik, did Father tell you what's going on?"

"He was vague. Mother is plotting something. We need to leave Ellnesari at once."

"And who is going to open a portal for us?" Saxon puts his hands on his hips, frowning.

"I will." Rikkon lifts his chin, almost daring the vampire to contradict him.

Saxon's eyes widen. I don't think he's used to seeing Rikkon behave with such confidence. I don't have anything against him, or Lucca, but those Bluebloods can be bullies if you let them walk all over you. As for Ronan, well, there's too much history there for me to ever warm up to him.

"If you're gonna do it, let's go. This place gives me the creeps." Solomon shivers, hugging himself.

"Right. Everyone, gather around. I can only do this once," Rikkon says.

We form a semicircle in front of him and wait.

"What do you think he's going to do?" Cheryl asks.

"Hopefully get us out of here," I reply.

A minute goes by, and nothing seems to happen. Rikkon has his eyes shut, and his brows are furrowed. Across from me, Saxon crosses his arms, and I can guess he's a second away from making a comment. But then a surge of magic emanates from Rikkon. I've never felt anything like it. It's different than the magic from the witches and Solomon. It feels stronger and old.

He extends his arm, and a ray of light whooshes from his outstretched hand. The light creates a ring big enough that we could walk through it. Cheryl gasps, stepping forward.

Rikkon finally opens his eyes and says, "You have to cross it now."

I hesitate. There's nothing in front of us but an opening with a blinding light that crackles with foreign magic.

"Do it!" he yells. "I can't hold it open for much longer."

"Oh, for fuck's sake. I'll go first." Solomon steps into the light and vanishes from sight.

Vivienne takes Lucca's hand, and together they step into the portal. Aurora glances at Miranda and tries to convince her to cross together with her and Saxon, but Miranda shakes her head.

"I'm crossing with Rik," she tells them.

"Come on, Rora. She'll be fine." Saxon tugs Aurora's hand.

I can see she's torn, but in the end, she lets Saxon steer her into the portal, keeping her eyes on Miranda until the light swallows her.

There's only Cheryl, Manu, Ronan, and me left, but something prevents me from stepping forward. My eyes immediately turn to Manu, and a sharp pain in my chest flares up suddenly.

"What are you waiting for? Can't you see the strain on Rikkon from keeping the portal open?" Miranda yells at us, frustrated.

"Come on, Karl." Cheryl tries to drag me forward, but I keep my feet firmly planted on the ground and my eyes glued on Manu.

The small hairs on the back of my neck are warning me something bad is going to happen. She locks her gaze with mine, and immediately I suspect something is afoot.

"You guys go ahead. I'll follow you," she says.

Cheryl pulls me toward the portal again, but I resist. Suddenly, a gust of wind pushes us forward. It's too strong, and there's nothing around for me to grab on. My skin tingles as we cross the portal, and then comes a drop. The portal opened high above the ground. My wolf instincts take over, and I land graciously on soft feet. My head is fuzzy though, and it takes me a second to recover from the trip.

It seems only Cheryl and I were able to not fall on our asses. Ronan is in a heap, cursing. I can't help the smirk that blossoms on my lips. He catches me staring and sneers.

"What are you looking at?"

"Nothing." My smile broadens.

He jumps back onto his feet and glances around. I know exactly who he's looking for because there's a big gaping hole in my chest now. Manu didn't come with us.

Rikkon and Miranda cross the portal next, though they don't drop out of the sky like we did but rather float down slowly.

"Couldn't you have brought us closer to the front door?" Saxon complains.

"The wards surrounding the mansion prevented it," Miranda replies.

"Where's my sister?" Lucca asks, frowning.

"She didn't want to come back." Miranda drops her chin and avoids making eye contact with him.

Manu is stubborn enough that if she didn't want to come back, no one could make her. Yet the anger that rushes through my veins can't be contained.

"You just left her behind?" I yell.

"She made her choice," Rikkon grits out. "She took off before we could force her through the portal. Going after her would mean getting stuck in Ellnesari. I couldn't do that to Miranda again."

"So now Manu is stuck there?" Lucca asks, his voice now dangerously low.

"For now." Rikkon nods.

"Why would she want to stay?" Vivi asks, hugging her middle.

"For revenge," Ronan replies, eyes growing dark. "She stayed in Ellnesari to kill Queen Maewe."

It makes sense. The Nightingale queen killed her mother and cursed Lucca and her. Nonetheless, my spine goes rigid as my irritation finds another mark. Ronan still acts like he's Manu's keeper and that rubs me raw. The old rivalry springs up again, making me see red.

Lucca whirls around and faces Ronan. "How do you know that? Did she tell you?"

"No, but I know Manu. The hate she feels for the queen has been festering all these years."

"Goddammit, that female!" I yank my hair back, not bothering to cover my frustration and anger.

"If that's her plan, it's foolhardy. Killing my mother is almost impossible," Rikkon says. "She'll get herself killed or worse."

"What's worse than dying?" Cheryl asks.

Vivi trades a meaningful glance with her brother. They probably believe there are worse fates in Ellnesari than biting the dust.

"You don't want to know," she replies.

"Fuck. There's nothing for it now. We have to go back and drag Manu's sorry ass home." Lucca looks pointedly at Rikkon.

"The magic my father shared with me was for a one-way ticket only," he says. "How did you cross into Ellnesari?"

"We used the Taluah Mirror, but unfortunately, it was destroyed in the process," Vivi replies, and we all turn to stare at Solomon.

His face twists into a scowl as he points his chubby finger at us. "Don't you dare give me that accusatory glance. I warned you that would happen."

I've heard enough. No one here will be able to find a solution to bring Manu back. It's up to me. I walk away from them and stare at the forest that surrounds the property.

"There has to be another way," I say, hating how desperate I sound. "We can't abandon Manu in Ellnesari."

"Why not?" Cheryl asks. "She had no problem abandoning *you*."

Her words feel like a dagger piercing my chest. She isn't wrong. I look over my shoulder. "You don't understand. You never will."

"I *do* understand, Karl. More than you know." She glances briefly in Ronan's direction before focusing on me again.

Hell. In that look, she confirmed what I suspected all along. She fell in love with that stupid-ass vampire. I can't even give her grief for being an idiot; I gave my heart to the wrong person too.

Ronan remains quiet, but his jaw hardens. What's his deal? He pretty much abandoned my sister after he turned her into an anomaly that almost cost her life. I can't for a second believe he cares about her.

Vivi steps closer to Lucca. "We'll find another way into Ellnesari, Luc. I promise."

"Vivi, you can't return," Rikkon tells her.

"Why the hell not?" She stands straighter. "I have my powers now."

"Exactly. Against Mom's wishes. She won't hesitate to come after you or Lucca."

Lucca pulls Vivi closer to him in a protective gesture. "She won't lay a hand on Vivi. I won't allow it."

Cheryl snorts. "No offense, dude, but what can you do against that female? Nothing. That's why going back to Ellnesari after Manu is a suicide mission."

"I don't care if it's a suicide mission. I'm going after her," I say.

Her gaze softens. "Karl—"

"Do you want your brother to die?" Ronan cuts Cheryl off. "If Manu dies in Ellnesari, so does Karl."

I clench my jaw to avoid barking at him. I don't want the douche to come to my defense. I also don't need him reminding Cheryl of what will most likely happen to me.

Her eyes flash bright yellow, and her canines elongate. "And that's the only reason she's kept her head attached to her body."

Cheryl's body trembles, and a moment later, she turns into a gray wolf and races off into the forest.

Damn it. I can't let her take off like that. In her current state of mind, she's bound to find trouble.

"You're back!" Vaughn says from the front door, smiling from ear to ear. "What happened?"

"There's much to discuss. Let's all head inside and cool off. We can't rush into things," Lucca replies.

"You go ahead and discuss all you want. I have to report back to Isadora," Solomon says.

I tune the rest of what he says out, too lost in my own head. My loyalties are split neatly in half. I'm torn between going after Cheryl and staying to find a way to rescue Manu.

Hell, there's only one thing I can do. I turn to Ronan.

"Go after my sister. Make sure she stays out of trouble."

His eyebrows shoot up. "Are you sure that's what you want?"

"It's not what I want, but it's high time you start taking responsibility for your actions."

His nostrils flare while his eyes sparkle with fury.

"As usual, you're talking out of your ass."

Lucca steps between us. "Enough!"

His intervention seems to snap Ronan out of his rage, his eyes going from murderous to guilty.

"I'll go after your sister, Karl. But you're wrong if you think I don't care about her."

Two

MANU

ITALY, 1520

I wait until it's midday to sneak out of my chambers. At this hour, not a soul is awake in my uncle's fortress. His soldiers and members of the Red Guard celebrated all night long after a victory against Tatiana's forces. I had every right to take part in the festivities, but the reason I'm now sneaking around didn't allow me to remain in the great hall past our meal.

My mother already suspects what ails me, but she hasn't said a word about it yet. My guess is—like everyone else in our family—she has too many problems occupying her mind.

My bare feet don't make a sound against the cold stone floor in the hallway, which augments the thump of my heart beating furiously inside my chest. I've avoided being in the same room alone with Ronan for a fortnight, but I can't evade him for much longer without making Lucca suspicious.

Ronan's chambers aren't far from mine. As a member of my brother's inner circle, he's earned the privilege of living close to the royal family. The short distance isn't enough to allow time for me to calm down. Although, I don't think anything can cure my anxiety.

By the time I stop in front of his door, my stomach is twisted into tight knots, and there's a lump in my throat constricting my airways. I curl my hands into fists, digging my nails into my soft palms until I pierce the skin.

I thought the pain would take my mind off what I have to do, but instead, the smell of blood only serves to alert Ronan that I'm standing outside his door. He knows my scent by heart.

My body freezes when I hear the sound of his footsteps approaching the door. The desire to flee is immense, but if I do, he'll come after me. It's not in his nature to let things go. He'd want to know why I came and then bolted.

The door's hinges creak loudly as he opens it. His tall and wide frame takes up most of the opening. A torch is lit behind him, making it hard to see his face even though vampires can see well at night.

"Manu, what are you doing here?" he asks in a low tone that hints at reproach.

"I need to speak with you."

He doesn't reply for a couple of beats. Then he looks fleetingly to the right, where Lucca's chambers are.

"He's passed out and won't rise from the dead until sundown," I say, answering the question I know is on his mind.

He lets out a heavy sigh. "You shouldn't be here."

"I shouldn't have done many things. But regret is not a malady I suffer from, unlike you."

His eyes flash red, but that's the only blatant reaction I get from him.

"Are you going to let me in or not?" I ask.

With a grunt, he opens the door wider and steps back. I walk in without looking in his direction, my spine so rigid that it could snap like a dried twig. I don't stop moving until I'm standing in the middle of his receiving room. It's still warm from the dying embers in the hearth. I focus on them for a moment, steeling myself before I tell Ronan the reason for my visit.

"Very well. You're here. What is it that you needed to tell me in the middle of the day while the fortress sleeps?"

The coldness in his voice would have made me sad before, but I have bigger concerns to worry about than being rejected by a male who I thought cared about me.

I turn around and meet his stern gaze.

"I'm with child," I blurt out.

Ronan's entire demeanor changes in an instant. He doesn't move; I dare say he's not even breathing. The silence stretches for several heartbeats, and the longer he keeps staring without saying a word, the more irritated I become.

"Aren't you going to say anything?"

"Who is the father?" he asks in a rough voice, as if it costs him to get the words out.

I blink fast as my mind tries to process what he just asked me.

"Who is the father?" I grit out. "You clearly jest."

"Are you saying it's mine?"

Each of his hurtful questions is akin to a punch to my stomach. My breathing becomes erratic, and it feels like the stone walls in the room are closing in. My gums ache as my fangs descend; my vision becomes tinged in red.

"How dare you ask me that?"

"You can't blame me. I've seen how you act around the males you come across. I can't hope you've only been with me."

"And how do I act around them? Please enlighten me, Ronan."

He clenches his jaw shut, knowing I set a trap and that no good ending will come if he answers my question. But I'm not interested in hearing the words come out of his mouth. I know exactly what he thinks about me. I'd seen his loathing stares whenever I gave my attention to a male who wasn't him. Yes, in the beginning, I flirted unabashedly to make him jealous. But all he did was stare at me in contempt. He never did what I wish he'd do —claim me as his. With time I realized he was never going to change how he felt about me. My infatuation with him lessened until it was gone. Then I found out about my condition, and here we are.

"Is it the way I smile at them? Bat my eyelashes at them? Laugh at their jokes? Does that make me a whore?"

"Don't act so offended. You've gone out of your way to show me how desirable every single male finds you. Your efforts weren't moot though. I know very well. I, after all, couldn't resist your charms despite my resolution to not cross that line with you."

"Was that the reason you ran out of my chambers so soon after the deed, as if the very sun was chasing after you?"

His eyes widen, and I can see remorse shining in them. "Manu, we both agreed that what happened between us was a mistake."

"Yes, it was. And now I have to live with the consequences. But don't worry, Ronan. I don't need to tell Lucca or the king that it's your child growing in my womb. Honestly, they won't care who the father is. False morality is not the way of our race."

"Have you gone mad? I'm not afraid of Lucca or your uncle. You don't have to go through it alone."

He takes a step forward as if a moment ago he hadn't accused me of lying with my uncle's entire battalion.

"You're right. But I'm choosing to." I spin around with every intention of rushing out of his chambers, but he grabs me by the arm and stops me.

"Let go of me if you wish to keep your arm attached to the rest of your body," I warn him through clenched teeth.

"I'm not going to let you walk out like this. We need to talk about it, Manu."

"You've said plenty." I glower. "I don't need your assistance in this matter."

"Bullshit. If you didn't want my involvement, you wouldn't have come here to tell me."

"I thought it was the honorable thing to do. I didn't expect you to act in the opposite way."

"You didn't say outright it was mine, and you can't blame me for asking."

"I might not be able to blame you, but I sure as hell resent you for it," I shout, making him wince. "Why in the world would I come here to tell you if you weren't the father?"

He passes a hand over his face and looks away. "I'm sorry. I shouldn't have listened to the rumors. Even Lucca believes in them."

"Lucca doesn't know me like I thought you did. You were my best friend." My voice cracks, and I hate myself for showing weakness in front of him.

Ronan notices and takes that opportunity to pull me into a hug. It's sudden, and I don't react immediately.

"I'm still your best friend." His voice is softer now, but instead of mollifying me, it does the opposite.

I push him back. "Too bad. You're no longer mine. I'm going back to my chambers, and you'd better not follow me, Ronan."

I don't wait for him to reply, just stride out of the room with my chin held high. He doesn't try to stop me this time or follow me. He does know me well—too well—and it hurts that I can no longer come to him as a friend. Too much has passed between us, too much hurt for us to go back to the way we were.

Moisture running down my cheeks surprises me. I'm not a crier. When I reach the bifurcation in the hallway, I don't take the corridor that would lead me back to my chambers. Instead I veer left and then down the spiraling stairs that will take me to the dungeons.

The farther down I go, the fouler the air becomes. No surprise, as this is where we keep our prisoners—soldiers from Tatiana's army. Their stay is never long, but their stench lingers. The cells are currently unoccupied; there were no survivors on the enemy's side this time.

Once I reach the bowels of the castle, I head to my private training room, which is on the opposite end of where the prison cells are. I found this spot when I was barely ten and wanted a place where I could hone my skills away from everyone's prying eyes. Pride has always been my biggest flaw. I didn't want to make a fool out of myself in front of Ronan and Lucca. No, I wanted to show off how good I was from the start.

Here, the stench isn't so thick. I walk over to the far wall and take my sword from its peg. The leather pommel has taken the shape of my hand already. I grasp it tighter, taking solace in the familiarity, then slash the air in an arc motion. That movement would have been followed by several others, but queasiness hits me first. I brace against the nearest wall and empty the contents of my stomach.

This is going to be a long seven months.

Three

KARL

ITALY, 1520

No sooner do I walk through the door than my mother whirls around and levels me with her stern gaze. It's quite a sight. The flames from the hearth make her wild red hair so bright, it looks like she has a ring of fire around her face. It matches the glowing ember of her eyes.

"Where have you been?"

Hell, I thought it'd be safe to return home and walk in through the front door. It's the middle of a moonless night, which means the majority of the wolves in our pack are probably sound asleep. The village sure was quiet on the way back home. I try to hide my flute behind my back, but her sharp eyes miss nothing.

She puts her hands on her hips. "You've been wasting your time at that human tavern again, haven't you?"

"I wasn't wasting my time," I retort, already making my way to the stairs.

"Where do you think you're going?" She moves fast and blocks my path.

"To bed." A yawn escapes me. "I'm exhausted."

"You're exhausted?" Her voice rises to a shriek, and I wince. "I've been consumed with worry."

"Why? The tavern in town isn't a dangerous place."

"Boy, you task me. There's conflict in our borders. Only one of our scouts returned, barely alive."

My eyes widen while my body turns rigid in the blink of an eye. "What happened?"

She twists her face into a scowl. "What do you think? Those wretched bloodsucking creatures happened."

"Vampires have come here? Why?"

"I don't know. To be honest, I don't think those parasites realize they've strayed far from their territory. They're too busy killing each other."

My blood runs cold. We've all heard the stories about the vicious war between two factions of the Blueblood vampires. My father, the alpha of our pack, has been sending scouts to gather more information for months. But the vampires' war didn't trouble me much. They'd never ventured this far north before.

"Where's Father?"

My mother's face becomes ashen. "He's taken his best fighters and gone to the borders. We cannot allow those savages to bring their destruction here."

Guilt pierces my chest. I'm one of his best fighters. I should have gone with him.

I set the flute on the nearby table and ask, "Where exactly has he gone?"

She shakes her head. "To Three-Headed Dragon Forest. But you can't go there alone. What if you come across a group of vampires? You can't fight them all alone. They'll tear you to shreds."

I narrow my eyes. "Only if they catch me."

The hurried steps of my sister coming down the stairs draw my attention away from Mom's worried face. She stops halfway down, wearing my woolen tunic and leather pants, not her sleeping gown.

"Karl, you're back."

Mom turns to her. "What in the world are you wearing, child?"

Cheryl comes down the rest of the way and stands before us. Her long hair is braided and tucked underneath the tunic. "I can't join Karl wearing the nonsense attire females are forced to wear in this pack. I'll need to undress fast before I shift."

"You're not coming with me," I say.

She snorts. "Try to stop me. I'm much faster than you."

Mom reaches for her arm and tugs roughly. "Take these clothes off immediately. I won't let you disgrace your father in this manner."

Cheryl pulls her arm free and glares through blazing ember eyes. "He needs the numbers. Surely he values the lives of his wolves more than his pride."

"Don't be so certain of that," I interject.

She whips her face to mine. "Are you going to take her side now? How about all that talk of wanting the females to have equal rights and responsibilities in the pack?"

My face becomes warmer as my irritation grows. I did say all those things, but now is not the time to speak of them. Cheryl, as usual, has terrible timing.

I shake my head. "I don't have time for this. If you want to come, I won't stop you."

"She's not going, Karl," Mom yells.

"Mother, we both know we wouldn't be able to stop Cheryl from coming even if we tied her up with wolfsbane-laced cords."

She gives our mother a victorious look. "He's right. You wouldn't."

Mom's nostrils flare as she fights to keep herself from shifting. We've seen it plenty of times growing up, she'd get angry and her wild side would show up. But as the dutiful wife of the alpha, she can't shift whenever her temper rises. It's not appropriate behavior. Females can only shift during the full moon or when in heat. Never mind that to deny our wolf nature is torturous. Cheryl dared me to do it when we were younger to make a point. From that day on, I vowed to change the rules that govern our society.

"If you insist on this madness, you'll have to deal with the consequences," Mom says. "Both of you."

"You worry too much, Mother." Cheryl steps closer to her and kisses her cheek.

Her expression softens, but only a little. Worry still shines in her eyes. She's been taught to act a certain way, and even if deep in her heart she knows it's not right, she's too afraid to fight for change.

As Cheryl steps back, I take her place and pull Mom into a hug. "I'll make sure Cheryl stays out of trouble. You have my vow."

"You shouldn't make vows you can't keep, son."

She's right, but I don't offer a comment. Instead, I kiss her forehead, and then I follow Cheryl out. It's the dead of winter, and even without any moonlight, I can see the white snow carpet that spreads before us. Our manor is at the edge of the forest, and Cheryl has already headed that way.

In silence, we remove our clothes and tuck them into the hollow of a nearby tree. It'd be easier if we took them off before heading out, but our mother wouldn't allow that. Decorum is expected. We're not humans, but we must behave like them.

We don't linger in our human form or we'd risk freezing to death. The change happens swiftly, and as soon as we're in wolf form, we break into a run. I let Cheryl lead until I pick up the scent of blood spilled.

"Slow down," I tell her telepathically.

I can sense the rebellion brewing in her mind, but she heeds my words. We continue at a much slower pace, on high alert for possible danger. The stench of blood increases, and now I can pick up the distinct notes. I smell vampire but also wolf.

A moment later, a howl of distress echoes in the distance, followed by several others. Before I can say anything, Cheryl takes off.

"Cheryl! Wait!"

"It's the pack. They're in trouble."

I run after her, but she's faster than me. Pushing my legs to the limit, I'm able to cut our distance short until a shadowed figure sprints between us, brandishing a broadsword that almost cuts me in half. I manage to swerve to the right and miss the steely blade by a hair. More vampires storm the area, and soon I lose track of Cheryl.

The vampire who almost cut me doesn't come after me. He's too busy now exchanging blows with his enemy. But just because I'm not their target doesn't mean I won't become collateral damage if I'm not careful.

I zigzag as I try to move away from the battleground. The howling and growling from my pack continue in the distance, which increases my urgency to get the hell out of here.

I finally see a straight path devoid of vampires and prepare to bolt when a female vampire steps into my line of vision. Like her counterparts, she's wearing armor, but hers is polished silver, not the dull gray of most. Her hair is dark and secured in a single braid save for the loose wisps framing her face. She looks fresh, as if she just joined the fray.

Her eyes scan the area, searching for something or someone. When she notices me just a few paces from her, she freezes and then holds her sword with both hands.

"You shouldn't be here, wolf."

I tense and prepare to attack. As beautiful as she is, I won't hesitate to sink my teeth into her lovely throat. A growl escapes my throat as I peel my lips back to show my sharp fangs. Her gaze narrows while she squares her jaw.

Another determined female being a thorn in my side. I must have offended a powerful deity in a previous life.

A battle cry breaks our staring contest. The female pivots to block an attack from a male twice her size. Her arms strain from the impact, and I fear she won't last long. I shouldn't care. Now that she's distracted, I can get out of here. Something compels me to ignore my instinct to flee though. Instead of running to aid my pack, I charge toward the duo of vampires.

It's only when I'm near them that I understand the female tricked her opponent into believing she was weaker than him. She pretends to lose her balance only to shove her sword into the male's gut. Such a wound won't kill, but it will slow down a vampire. Faster than lightning, she pulls her sword free and then finishes the job, decapitating the male.

His head and body fall in different directions, but there's no time to appreciate her handiwork. More vampires come at her, and now she's overwhelmed. As good as she is with her sword, she can't possibly fight them all at once.

Before reason returns to my brain, I pounce on the nearest bloodsucker, sinking my teeth into his jugular. His foul blood almost makes me gag, but I keep working my teeth through muscle and bone until his head snaps off.

During the time I was busy dispatching my vampire, the female killed three. She's breathing hard as she stares at me, a vision of death bathed in blood. Her moment of distraction delays her reaction when the next assault comes. A vampire who I hadn't noticed approaches from behind with his sword raised high, ready to deliver the killing blow.

I want to shout a warning, but in this form, all I can do is bark. She turns in time to avoid the worst—death by decapitation —but the blade cuts through her collarbone. The scent of her blood ignites something in my core, a primal instinct to protect. Wolves don't react this viscerally over spilled blood, so I can't begin to understand what's happening to me.

She's hurt, but she's not cowed and continues to fight. The male is vicious and takes pleasure in seeing her in pain. It tinges my vision red; it makes me want to shred him into pieces. When I find an opening, I jump on his back, trying to find his neck. But unlike the other male I killed, this one's armor protects his neck better, and my teeth only meet metal.

With ease, he rips me off his back and throws me against a

tree. I whimper as white-hot pain shoots up my spine. I think I hear the female calling me a fool, but I'm momentarily dizzy.

A horn sounds off in the distance, and to my surprise, the ugly bloodsucker takes off and disappears into the dark forest. I spring back to my feet, wincing in pain, and take stock of who is left alive.

I count a few males, but they're hurt and moving sluggishly, just like I am. I'm in no condition to fight, and yet I don't make a motion to run away when the female approaches me. Blood splatters have covered her face and the front of her armor. It doesn't make her any less stunning.

"Why did you help me?" she asks, then shakes her head. "You'd better find the rest of your pack. You don't want to be around when my un—ugh!" She doubles over, hugging her middle.

Her face is twisted in agony as she staggers forward to brace her hand against the tree behind me.

Did she suffer another injury I missed?

I rub against her leg, the only thing I can think of doing. I wish I could shift and ask her what's wrong, but that'd be the second stupid thing I'd do tonight.

She glances down to stare into my eyes. I think she's trying to read my mind. A moment later, she looks over her shoulder. The horn we heard earlier sounds again, closer.

"I can't be here," she grits out. "And neither can you."

Four

MANU

ITALY, 1520

The pain in my lower abdomen hits me out of nowhere, crippling me to the point that I need to brace against the tree. This happens under the watchful gaze of the wolf shifter. I'm taken by surprise when he rubs his side against my belly. I don't know what to make of it.

My uncle's horn sounds again, closer this time, and I know I have to get out of here.

I felt ill earlier in the evening, and he ordered me not to come tonight. I haven't told him yet that I'm expecting a baby, but if he sees me now, he won't be pleased. Ronan will be furious for certain, and he might end up revealing my secret.

Another cramp steals my breath. I can't let them find me in this state.

"I can't be here." I lock gazes with the wolf. "And neither can you."

I summon every ounce of strength I have left and break into a run. The wolf shifter follows me. That's not what I had in mind when I told him he needed to go. Moments before he crossed my path, he wanted to find his pack mates, I'm sure of it. So why is he following me now?

It's hard to maintain my speed when it feels like a sword is embedded in my stomach. I only slow down when I can no longer hear the king's approaching forces. Tonight's attack by Tatiana's soldiers wasn't expected. After we decimated her forces two nights ago, we believed we'd earned a reprieve. It's clear now that the small army we faced was only a ruse to give us a false sense of victory.

I fall to my knees and then curl into a ball, fighting to keep my cries bottled inside. I've never felt such terrible agony before. The snow-covered ground quickly turns my body to ice, and I begin to shiver.

The crunching of paws nearby tells me the wolf is still with me. I turn in time to see him shift into a tall, naked man with broad shoulders and a body corded with muscles. His red hair is wavy and wild, which suits him.

"What are you doing? You'll freeze to death."

He crouches next to me. "I can't help you in my wolf form. What ails you?"

His green eyes bore into mine, and I feel the power of that connection even through the haze of pain.

"I-I don't know."

His nostrils flare, and then his gaze switches to my legs. "You're bleeding."

"What?" I run my hand down my inner thigh and find the fabric soaked through. My heart sinks with the realization of what's happening to me. "No."

"I need to take you home."

Fear grips my insides. If any of my uncle's soldiers catch me being carried by a naked shifter, they'll attack first and ask questions later. Vampires don't play well with the other supernatural species, something I never understood.

"It's too far. You'll freeze to death beforehand."

He picks me up and rises. The movement doubles my pain,

but I don't make a sound. Instead, I press my cheek against his chest, finding it warm despite the frosty weather. His heartbeat is steady, and I focus on it to try to forget what's happening to me. I don't know where he thinks he's taking me, but I don't ask. My instincts are telling me I can trust him with my life.

"There's a cabin ahead. I don't sense anyone inside," he tells me after a while.

"Is it abandoned?"

"By the looks of it, I'd say yes."

Reluctantly, I lean away from his heat and turn to see what he's referring to. A bubble of laughter rises up my throat. The pain is already making me lose my mind.

"You call that a cabin?"

The stone building shows the charred mark of a fire, and one wall is leaning in perilously.

"It has a roof and four walls, so yes, I'm calling that a cabin."

He strides forward and enters the place as if he were a king and this was his palace. The stench of burned wood is still strong, but whoever lived here previously managed to put out the fire before it destroyed everything.

"I have to lay you down so I can build a fire."

Another sharp tug in my womb makes me forget where we are. I barely notice when he carefully lowers me to the dusty ground. It's damn cold. This is not a good sign. I'm dressed from head to toe. How can he stand the low temperature when he's naked like that?

I once again make myself smaller while I watch him work. He gathers pieces of charred furniture and breaks them into smaller bits as if they were twigs. I shouldn't notice how his muscles flex or how attractive he is, but I'm not blind.

After he gathers enough wood to burn, he proceeds to start the fire. It doesn't take long for him to manage it, and I'm once again surprised by his ability to do so with the scarce resources at his disposal.

The flames turn his hair even redder, making him look like a sun god. I can't help but be amused by the irony. A vampire being helped by a creature who resembles the very thing that could kill us.

He turns to me, frowning. "How are you?"

"Fine."

He shakes his head before he walks over and sits next to me. "You're lying. You don't need to mask your pain on my account. I know you're a fierce warrior."

"How do you know I'm lying?"

"I can tell." He brings his knees up and hugs his legs while his gaze remains trained on the fire.

"You must be terribly cold. Why don't you shift back into your wolf form?"

"I'll be warm soon enough. And I'd rather retain my arms for now, in case you need my assistance."

A strange fuzzy feeling spreads through my chest. Save for my family, I'm not used to kindness from others.

"Why are you helping me? I'm a vampire. I thought wolves hated my kind."

He chuckles. "True. I don't know why I'm helping you. My pack was in distress, and I chose to assist a bloodsucking fiend who brought war to our lands."

I don't detect sarcasm or anger in his tone, but I still feel guilty. He's not wrong. The war between my uncle and Tatiana has affected more than just the vampires.

"I'm sorry."

He glances at me. "You mean that, don't you?"

I close my eyes for a moment. "I do. I hate this war, but we can't let Tatiana and her followers kill at will. We need to stop that bitch."

"Even at the cost of your unborn child?"

His question feels like a dagger piercing my chest. Tears prickle my eyes, and for the first time since meeting this male, I feel animosity toward him.

"You don't know anything about me," I grit out.

"You're right. I don't. I'm sorry. My comment was unwarranted. Is there anything I can do?"

His apology is heartfelt. I can see it in his eyes, and it makes me want to cry. A lump gets lodged in my throat.

"I don't think there's anything you can do."

"Are you still in pain?"

"Yes, but not as intense as before."

We don't speak for a couple of heartbeats, but we also don't break eye contact. It's strange how comfortable I am in his company.

"Females of my kind aren't allowed to shift when they're expecting," he says suddenly.

"Why?"

"For one, it's too risky. But also, our society views them as inferior and weak."

I frown. "Do you also believe that?"

"No."

Another cramp distracts me. I try not to grimace, but I don't think I succeed. He touches my arm in a comforting gesture.

"I should have taken you back to your family," he says.

"I would have fought you tooth and nail if you'd tried."

"Why? Are they awful to you?"

"No, but my uncle didn't know I was with child."

"You said *was*. You don't know if it's in the past. Maybe the little nugget is a fighter, like his mother." The corners of his lips tug upward, the shade of a smile that makes my chest tight with the feeling of longing.

I look away, trying to hide the moisture that's gathered in my eyes. "There's too much blood."

"I'm sorry."

A rogue tear escapes the corner of my eye. I hastily wipe it off. "You have no reason to be. You don't know me, and you didn't cause this."

"I can still feel sadness for you."

I don't want his pity, so I glare at him, but I can't hold my anger for too long.

"What's your name?" I ask.

"Karl Eriksson."

"Well, Karl Eriksson, you don't need to stay with me. Go after your—"

The sound of boots crunching on the snow outside cuts me off.

Karl jumps to his feet, his body now coiled with tension. A heartbeat later, Ronan appears at the door of the cabin, a menace in armor and steel.

"Step away from her," he growls, raising his sword.

"Ronan, stop it." I try to sit up, but the pain returns with a vengeance. I let out a wail and fold into myself.

He roars and charges.

Damn everything to hell. I have to stop this madness.

"No! He helped me."

My outburst comes too late, and he doesn't stop in time. Karl jumps out of the path of his lethal blow, shifting into wolf midair. There's no place to run save through the front door, which Ronan is blocking. Besides, the reach of his arm is long. It won't take long before he gets Karl into a corner and cuts him in half.

With a grunt, I get onto my knees and grab the end of Ronan's cape. "Stop it."

He freezes and looks down. "What did he do to you?"

"He saved me."

Karl growls, ready to attack Ronan, but unlike the male staring at me wide eyed, he waits.

"He's a beast," Ronan retorts. "You can't trust him."

I almost wish Karl would snap and attack Ronan, but the world suddenly dims until there's nothing but darkness.

Five

KARL

ITALY, 1520

I don't know who this male is, but he clearly isn't here to harm her. I can't say the same thing about his intentions toward me. She tries to stop him, and then she collapses. I almost shift back into human form but stop short when the vampire turns his back to me and picks her up in his arms. There's familiarity in that gesture, and my wolf rebels against it. I'm acting as if we're mated, which is madness. She's a vampire, for heaven's sake.

It's hard to fight my wolf's instinct to attack the vampire though. I almost succumb to it, but then I hear a howl not far from us. The small hairs on my back stand on end. That's Cheryl's call. She's looking for me.

I spare another glance at the female in the vampire's arms, wrestling with my feelings. The male seems to have forgotten about me as he caresses her cheek. He cares about her. She'll be safe with him, but I don't want to leave, which means I should.

Before my wolf gains control, I rush out the cabin's door. My heart seems to shatter into pieces with each step I take.

Cheryl howls again, and I veer toward the sound. When I'm close enough, I send her a telepathic message.

"I'm coming."

"Where have you been?"

"I got busy fighting my way through a group of vampires."

I finally spot her running, and I'm glad to see she isn't hurt.

"Did you find Father and the others?" I ask.

"Yes, they've returned to the village. Some got hurt. I stayed behind to look for you."

"Did he see you?"

There's a moment of silence, which doesn't bode well.

"He did, didn't he?"

"Yes. But I don't want to talk about it now." She joins me at my side and then says, *"What's that smell?"*

"You have to be more specific than that."

"You reek of vampire."

Ah hell. It didn't even occur to me that Cheryl would be able to pick up the female's scent.

"Why are you surprised? I was fighting them."

"Did they attack you?"

"Yes, the vampires fighting King Raphael's forces. They're bad news."

"Don't be a fool. They're all bad news, Karl."

It'd be pointless to try to convince her that not all of them are bad, especially when we come across the carnage they left behind while they were trying to kill one another.

I don't say another word during the rest of our trip back to our village. My thoughts are consumed by the female vampire. I've never met anyone like her. I'm glad Cheryl can't hear my thoughts unless I let her in. She would not approve of my sudden obsession. I'm not sure I do either.

When we finally arrive at the spot where we hid our clothes, we shift back and get dressed as quickly as possible. Cheryl's face is grim as we walk toward the manor. If our father saw her, a punishment is in store for her. She knew what she was getting into, but I can't help feeling guilty that I let her tag along.

At the door, I step in front of her. "Let me go in first."

"Okay."

The scene I encounter as I step foot inside brings bile to my mouth. There are two unshifted wolves lying near the fireplace, covered in lacerations. Our mother is cleaning the wound of one while my father and his beta stand nearby, watching her work and bearing similar grim expressions. They both turn when we enter, revealing a big gash on my father's cheek.

"Where have you been?" he asks.

"Trying to make my way back from the fight," I say.

He narrows his eyes and then switches his hard gaze to Cheryl. "Go to the kitchen and grab another bucket to fill with snow. We need more hot water."

"Yes, Father." She hurries to comply.

My sister is a rebel, but she knows when to play the obedient daughter.

"Is that Sven and Gale?" I ask.

"Yes."

"Did they get caught between the two armies?"

Dietrich, my father's beta, snorts. "This wasn't an accident. They were hunted down for sport."

My heart becomes tight. "By whom?"

"Who do you think?" my father snarls. "Those blood-sucking vampires. I wish they'd go ahead and kill one another already."

"I know that's the vampires' doing, but which faction? King Raphael's or Tatiana's?"

"Does it matter? They're all awful," Dietrich retorts, then turns to my father. "I think it's high time we reach out to the dragon shifters. We can't let the vampires destroy our world."

"Good luck finding them," I say. "They want nothing to do with the rest of the supernatural community."

"That's not true, Karl," Father replies. "While you were busy fooling around with your human friends, a messenger from Larsson van Praag made contact."

My eyes widen as I digest the news. Larsson van Praag is the savage dragon king from the northern lands. His legend precedes him.

"When did that happen?"

"A fortnight ago."

"Why didn't you tell me?"

My father trades a look with Dietrich, then glances at me. "Because it wasn't the time. No one in the pack save for Dietrich and your mother knew. I didn't want to alarm the wolves. Dragons aren't famous for working well with other supernaturals. An alliance with them could cost us more than facing the vampires alone."

"I don't think we should. I don't trust those scaly beasts one bit," Mom interjects.

Dietrich watches her with a scowl. Most females in our pack wouldn't dare speak like that to their mates, but my father isn't as backward as most males. He won't go easy on Cheryl though.

"We might not have a choice if the vampires turn their war on us."

Cheryl returns with the bucket of snow and crouches next to Sven. They're close friends, although I know he hopes to be more than that one day. Cheryl is either oblivious or she's pretending to be.

"Why can't they shift?" she asks.

"They're in too much pain to do so." Mom dumps some of the snow in the cauldron by the fire. "All we can do now is clean their wounds and wait for them to heal on their own."

Sven whimpers when Mom rubs a wet cloth over a gash on his hind leg.

Cheryl takes the cloth from her. "Let me do it."

I watch the scene for a couple of beats, thinking that it wouldn't be a terrible thing if Cheryl and Sven married. He's kind to her. He wouldn't give her grief for her forward ways.

"We need to share the dragons' message with the rest of the pack, Melker," Dietrich says.

"I know. Tomorrow. Let's all rest tonight. Go home, Dietrich."

"Yes, Alpha." He nods and then walks out, but not before he spares me a loathing stare.

He never liked me, but now he's not even trying to hide it. He'd probably slash my throat if he suspected I helped a vampire tonight. Out of all the wolves in our pack, his hatred for the vampires runs deeper than the sea.

MANU

When I wake up, I'm back in my chambers, tucked in bed. The fire rages in the hearth, bathing everything in orange. My throat is dry; I haven't eaten anything in a day.

My mother appears in my line of sight and walks over to the side of the bed.

She places a hand against my forehead. "How are you feeling, darling?"

"Like hell."

My brain is fuzzy, so it takes me a while to remember everything that's happened in the past day or so. When I do, there's a sharp tug in my chest. I press my hands against my lower belly.

"Did I...?"

My mother's expression says it all. "I'm sorry, Manu. By the time Ronan brought you in, there was nothing we could do."

"We?"

"The High Witch and I. Raphael and Lucca don't know."

I look away and focus on the dancing flames. "What did Ronan say?"

"He didn't have to say anything. I wasn't born yesterday, child."

"How was he after he found out about what happened?"

She frowns. "Distraught, naturally. He's a male of honor, Manu."

"You wouldn't think that if you had witnessed his reaction when I told him the baby was his."

I didn't intend to sound bitter, but the feeling sneaks into my tone, nonetheless.

"He's a male, and they're foolish more times than not."

"That sounds like a terrible excuse. 'I'm an asshole because I have a penis.'"

"It's not an excuse. It's an explanation. You do with that what you will. You can spend the rest of your life resenting him, or you can move on."

Mom is right. Resenting Ronan won't do me any good, but holding on to it right now is the only thing keeping me from feeling the brunt of my reality. I lost my baby. Even if I wasn't going to be with Ronan, I wanted our child.

"It doesn't matter now. The only tie we had is gone."

She raises a brow. "The only tie? You were friends before."

"I don't think we are anymore. I can't go back to the way we were."

Mom pats my arm. "Time heals everything. It's providential that we have a long existence."

"If Tatiana doesn't kill us all. I faced Boone in the forest."

Mom's face goes ashen. Boone is Tatiana's deranged son. He's known for his viciousness and cruelty.

"Did he strike you in your belly? Was that what happened?"

Her eyes burn with intensity. If that had happened, she would hunt that bastard down and kill him with her bare hands.

"No, he didn't. I think my miscarriage would have occurred even if I hadn't gone into battle. I didn't exhaust myself out there. I swear."

Mom's gaze becomes sad. She looks away and stares at the flames. "I lost my first baby as well."

"You did? How come you never told me that?"

She sighs loudly. "That's not something most females like to talk about. As for me, I was riddled with guilt. I didn't leave my chambers for months. I kept thinking I lost my child because I'd done something wrong."

"What made you change your mind?"

"Solomon."

"The first familiar?" I question.

"Yes. He came to see me when none of the High Witch's spells or the healers' potions worked."

"What did he do?"

"He was brutally honest with me. I had two choices: wither away and join my unborn child, or get out of that bed and join the living."

"And that speech worked?"

She smiles ruefully. "It angered me so much that I did get out of bed so I could kick him out of my chambers. So I suppose it did work. Months later, I got pregnant with Lucca."

I take a deep breath. "I'm not quite ready to get pregnant again. This time around was unexpected."

"You're young. There will be time for that, preferably when Tatiana is no longer an issue."

"You mean when she's dead?"

Mom's gaze darkens. "Yes. Now, are you hungry? I can send for some blood."

"I don't think I can eat now. Perhaps later."

"Very well, then. Now rest, dear. Sundown won't be for a few more hours."

I watch her leave and then close my eyes, but as tired as I am, I know sleep will elude me. I think about my mother's confession, then try to picture myself with child again. Strangely, I don't rebel against the idea, but it's the sun god wolf shifter who I see by my side.

Six

MANU

Things at the mansion are tense as ever. I can feel the walls closing in as the problems pile up, getting ready to blow. I can't take Lucca's shadowed gaze or Ronan's foul mood. Even Saxon's demeanor has changed. We all know we're at the verge of extinction, but no one has the guts to speak about it out loud.

Lucca doesn't want us taking unnecessary risks, so all outings are forbidden. Tonight, however, I ignored his orders. I was ready to snap. Now I'm standing in front of Havoc, debating if I should go in or not. For years, this has been the place where I come to satiate my hunger for blood and sex.

My hesitation puzzles me. I can't remember the last time I didn't need to use sex to forget my problems.

That's obviously a lie. I can remember vividly, and the pain of the memory is as sharp as ever. For centuries, I did a phenomenal job keeping that part of my life locked in a vault, but my uncle had to meddle and bring back the one person capable of making me lose my mind.

Anger replaces the pain, and I square my shoulders and cross the street. The humans waiting in line all turn to stare at me. I'm a sight to them, I just don't know if they think I'm a dream or a nightmare in heels. The bouncer at the door nods as I walk past him. I don't slow down until I'm standing at the edge of the dance floor.

I glance over, trying to decide what I'm in the mood for tonight. The crowd is a mix of humans and vampires, skewing heavily on the human side. Even with the current turmoil in Salem, humans are still flocking here, hoping to be a meal and a hookup for our kind. My eyes land on a set of identical twins dancing with an ordinary female. She isn't a Blueblood, but she's attractive, I suppose.

While I try to decide if I want a threesome with the duo, one of them catches me staring. His eyes widen in recognition, and then he whispers in his brother's ear. Now both are looking at me. That doesn't go unnoticed by their companion. She turns in my direction and glowers. She knows all I need to do is snap my fingers and the Wonder Twins will come running to me. Her animosity serves as the deciding factor for me. I wasn't sure if I wanted a threesome tonight—now I do.

I'm about to steal her snacks when I sense his presence nearby. *Son of a bitch.* I turn around and search for him. It doesn't take long for me to see Karl's red hair in the crowd. Taller than most here, he's easy to spot. He's coming straight to me, which means he's looking for me.

His presence kills my buzz. It's bad enough that my uncle shoved Karl down my throat and forced him to move in the institute. I thought I'd be rid of him now that we're back in the mansion, but it seems he's intent on being a wad of gum stuck to my shoe.

I don't wait until he joins me, just veer toward the bar. However, I don't get halfway there before he grabs my arm.

"Manu, wait."

The contact sends shivers down my spine. I can't believe after all these years, I still react this way to his touch. Annoyed, I yank my arm free from his grasp.

"What do you want, Karl?"

"Lucca told me you left the mansion."

"Oh, so you're his bitch now too?"

He growls. "Watch your mouth, Manu."

"Am I lying? All it took was an order from my uncle to bring you back by my side, despite what I did to you those centuries ago."

I try to ignore how painful that moment still is to me. It was the worst day of my life. I can't let Karl suspect it though. He needs to believe I'm a heartless, heinous bitch who doesn't give a flying fuck about him.

"He does not give me orders," he grits out. "No one from your kind does. If you weren't so self-centered, you would know that."

"Whatever lies you tell yourself." I walk around him and head to the exit. His presence here ruined my plans.

It would be too much to hope he'd leave me alone. The pest follows me, and my irritation escalates to eleven. He's always been stubborn, but he's taking it to the next level. How many times must I reject him, treat him badly until he tells me to fuck off and die?

Sometimes, that's exactly what I think I deserve. What keeps me from meeting the sun is the knowledge that if I die, he dies. I can't have that on my conscience, even after death.

If only I could tell him that everything I've done and continue to do is because of what he means to me.

"Stop following me," I say.

"I will once you get some sense in your head and return to the mansion."

I whirl around and poke him in the chest. "I don't fucking need you to babysit me, Karl."

His face twists into a scowl. "I beg to differ. You were

kidnapped and framed for the murder of a dragon not too long ago, or have you forgotten that already?"

Now it's my turn to glower. "No, I haven't forgotten. You seriously don't believe I'm going to fall for another trap, do you?"

"You don't have the best track record, sweetheart. Now be a good girl and go home. I'm sure Gerard can order a snack for you to drink from and fuck."

His words have so much venom in them that they make me wince.

"You're an asshole."

His lips curl into a cruel grin. "Yes, but only to those who deserve it."

Being this close to him, it's impossible to remain unaffected by his hatred. My throat constricts while my body shakes from head to toe. My resolve is crumbling faster than lightning, and I can't allow that to happen. I have to keep my distance.

Even if he denies being at the service of my uncle and Lucca, I know if one of them orders him to go away, he will. Lucca won't take my side unless I tell him the truth, which I can't. He'd hate me too if he knew. The only person who can remove Karl from my life is my uncle.

Now that I have a solid plan, it's a little easier to forget the agony in my chest. I step away from Karl and then whirl around.

"Are you going home?" he asks.

"No."

He curses under his breath and then follows me.

"Do I need to bind you and take you back by force?"

I laugh without humor. "You can try."

No, no. What are you doing, Manu, goading him like that? I know Karl would follow through, but I can't let him put his hands on me. That would have disastrous consequences.

"Manu, I swear to God...."

"I'm going to see my uncle. Follow me if you must. I don't care."

Seven

KARL

SALEM, A WEEK BEFORE ELLNESARI

When Lucca called, I almost told him he should fetch his sister himself. I'm sick and tired of dealing with the bloodsuckers. But then I remembered how much has fallen on his shoulders in such a short period of time, and I bit my tongue. Plus, I can't hate his kind on account of my issues with Manu. That would put me in the same category as Dietrich, the son of a bitch responsible for so much grief in my life.

I shake my head. I haven't thought about that vermin in a long time, but I guess the forced proximity to Manu has reopened several wounds.

Swallowing my pride, I follow her to her car. I didn't drive here since I was close enough to Havoc when Lucca called that it was faster if I simply shifted. Gone are the days when we have to worry about clothes. Thanks to a spell, we don't have to stash them somewhere and then parade naked afterward.

She turns around when she realizes I intend to ride with her.

"What do you think you're doing?"

"Tagging along. I don't feel like chasing after you. I've done that plenty in my existence."

She scoffs. "No one forced you."

"I beg to differ. But whatever, I'm not getting into that argument with you again." I open the passenger door and slide in before she can say another word.

She gets behind the steering wheel and glares at me for a couple of seconds. I keep my gaze forward, ignoring her. She's always hated when people do that to her, so I take pleasure in annoying her further. It's better than the feeling of utter hopelessness that always takes over me when I see her face.

"I don't remember when you turned into this pathetic creature. Have you no pride?"

My nostrils flare. She's goading me, poking my sore spot. When she betrayed me and then sent me away, she destroyed me in more ways than one. I gave her my life, pledged my soul to her, only for her to toss it away as if it were garbage.

I shrug. "If you're going to speak with your uncle about me, then I have to be there. We both want the same thing, after all, to never have to see each other again."

"That's right. If what you said is true, if you're not following his orders, then all you have to do is pack your shit and leave Salem."

I laugh without humor. "Sorry, darling. You're not the queen of this town. Salem is my home. I have friends and family here. The only person I don't want to see is you."

When she doesn't offer me an angry retort, I glance at her. I don't expect to catch the glint of hurt shining in her yellow eyes. She looks away quickly and turns the engine on. I have to force my attention back to the road instead of staring at her profile. It doesn't matter that she's showing emotion; it doesn't change the past.

We don't speak during the ride to King Raphael's mansion, which is hidden from everyone thanks to a powerful spell cast by the High Witch. Only those cleared to cross his domain are able to find the place. Manu blazes through the barrier without slowing down. When she parks in front of the building, Mauricio Libell, King Raphael's familiar, is already waiting for us at the front door. Built like a mountain, the male is as imposing as they come, which doesn't surprise me, considering who he's linked to. I wonder how he feels about being tied to a vampire who might die soon.

"You're not expected, Manu," he says in his baritone voice as soon as she exits the car.

"Do you think I care about that?" She strides forward, not bothered that Mauricio is blocking the entrance.

"You should care. The king is in no condition to deal with your drama."

She stops in front of him, lifting her chin to properly glower at the male. "I'm not here to bring drama. I legit need to speak with him. It's important."

He looks over her head. "You brought your familiar. Don't tell me you're not here to cause drama."

"Manu wants to check on her uncle," I cut in. "Are you seriously going to deny her entrance?"

Her spine becomes taut—a reaction to me coming to her defense. Mauricio misses it since he was too busy glaring at me.

"Very well. But if you cause him any distress, I'll toss you out on your asses."

Instead of stepping aside, he turns around and walks in first. He doesn't outrank Manu or Lucca, but he doesn't give a fuck about proper protocol.

I follow Manu inside the grand house, which is indeed fit for a king. The floor in the foyer is white marble, so polished I can see my reflection in it. This isn't my first time here, but I'm always hit by awe. Tonight, there's no time to gawk at the house's splendor. Manu is in a hurry to see her uncle. She practically sprints down the stairs to the basement where the king's chambers currently are. The mansion has shutters that automatically lower with sunrise, but the king himself chose to move to a more secure location on account of his disease. He also ordered Mauricio to keep him locked up. He issued himself a prison sentence.

It's hard to imagine that such a powerful vampire would be forced to that extreme. But after he tried to kill Saxon in battle, it's a precaution that needed to be taken.

Manu stops in front of the locked door and knocks. "Uncle?"

When no answer comes, she reaches for the lock, but I catch her wrist, stopping her. "Maybe Mauricio should be here as well."

Her eyebrows arch. "My uncle won't attack me."

"You don't know that."

"He's right, Manu. He's having trouble remembering things," Mauricio pipes up.

"What about you? Aren't you concerned he'll turn on you too?"

The male's face shows nothing, not even an ounce of worry. "No."

I let go of her wrist when I realize I was still holding it and step back. Manu moves the other way, giving Mauricio space to unlock the door. My fingertips still tingle from the contact with her skin, and I wonder if she felt the same.

Stop it, Karl. You can't indulge these thoughts.

Mauricio pushes the heavy steel door open and walks in. "My king?"

No answer comes forth, but the male strides into the dark room without fear. I make a motion to follow him, my ingrained instinct to protect Manu projecting at full force, but she cuts in front of me.

"Uncle Raphael?" she calls him again, and finally we hear an annoyed grunt.

"What do you want?" He steps forward, eyes gleaming red, which is never a good sign when it comes to vampires.

My body tenses, and ahead of me, I sense the same reaction from Mauricio. Things can get dicey in a split second.

"I came to see how you're doing," she says.

"Don't lie to me!" he snarls, revealing his fangs.

"I'm not lying." Manu's voice is feeble, laced with pain. It twists my guts.

Faster than lightning, he grabs a chair and hurls it in her direction. She dodges, and it crashes against the far wall in bits of furniture.

"Get out!" he yells.

His breathing is coming out in bursts. It doesn't take a genius to understand he's holding on to his control by a thread.

"Come on, Manu." Mauricio steps closer to her.

She doesn't pay him any attention. Her focus is solely on King Raphael.

He steps forward, taking on an aggressive stance. His nails have turned into claws, and the power emanating from him is impossible to miss. Manu doesn't seem to notice—or care—about the danger.

"For fuck's sake," I say under my breath.

I grab her arm and drag her with me out of the room.

"Let me go, Karl," she says, but there's no fight in her body.

Mauricio follows close behind and quickly locks the door once more. He doesn't move as he stares ahead, but he does say, "You can't come see him anymore unless you have a cure for his ailment."

"I didn't think the disease had progressed that fast," she says.

"He wasn't like that yesterday." Mauricio turns to us, his dark gaze troubled. "If the magic of the Nightingales isn't restored, I'm afraid we'll be losing our king soon."

My throat becomes tight. I knew things were taking a turn for the worse, but I didn't imagine they were developing so quickly.

I glance at Manu's stricken face. Her eyes are brighter now thanks to her unshed tears. She locks her gaze with mine, and then a second later, she bolts up the stairs.

I should leave her alone, but I find myself going after her. She's outside, standing next to her car when I catch up with her. Her shoulders are shaking, and her face is hidden behind her hands.

"Manu," I say as I touch her arm.

She pulls away in a jerky movement. "Leave me alone, Karl."

"We'll find a way to save your uncle."

She turns to glare at me. "We? What makes you think you have any part in this?"

I shake my head. "Fine. Be like that. Push everyone who cares about you away."

Her eyes widen. "You can't possibly still care about me."

Shit. I said too much.

"I wasn't referring to myself."

The lie is pointless, but I stick to it. However, I can't remain in her company for a second longer. I close my eyes and surrender myself to the wolf before I run away from my personal hell.

Eight

MANU

ITALY, 1520

Unlike my mother, it didn't take me months of solitude and a sermon from Solomon to propel me back to normal life. The sadness still lingers in my chest though, and I don't think it will ever go away. But I can't wallow in self-pity when there's a war going on.

It's been a week since I lost my child. I haven't spoken to Ronan yet, but it wasn't for lack of him trying to get me alone. In truth, there's nothing he can say in this moment that will make me feel better about the situation.

I think about the wolf shifter often though. So much that it's becoming an obsession I don't plan to give up—as long as I only see him in my memories. Seeking him out would be unwise and dangerous for both of us.

After the surprise attack by Tatiana's forces, my uncle decided to call a council meeting to discuss our next move. The tension is undeniable in the war room as we wait for the last guest to arrive. Sitting at the long table are my uncle at the head, Lucca on his right side, and my mother on his left. I'm sitting next to her while Ronan is next to Lucca, meaning I'm right across from him. I make a point to not lock gazes with him even though I can feel the intensity of his stare.

"What did you do to my sister to piss her off?" Lucca asks under his breath.

I don't know why he bothered whispering when he knows I can hear him perfectly.

"He's done nothing. Mind your own business," I hiss.

He narrows his eyes at me but knows better than to push the issue while Uncle Raphael and members of his Red Guard are watching. Those males may not be Bluebloods, but they are some of the most skilled and powerful vampires in the land, and we don't want to appear childlike to them. Lucca hopes to one day train with the Red Guard, hence why he's biting his tongue.

Uncle Raphael is holding a goblet of blood but makes no attempt to of drink from it. His eyes are unfocused but also troubled. The war with Tatiana has been going on for far too long, and with each year, she seems to gain more allies.

The door to the chamber opens and in comes Derek Blackwater, a handsome and roguish made vampire who has belonged to my uncle's inner circle since I can remember. His position of influence is unusual. Most made vampires are considered second-class citizens and never rise in the scales of influence.

No one can deny the power of Derek Blackwater though, and the few who questioned his status didn't live to tell the tale.

"Good evening, my king." The male bows his head.

"Derek. I'm glad to see you."

"Perhaps you won't be after I share the news I have."

The tension seems to grow tenfold. Lucca and I exchange a glance, and then he looks at Ronan, who has a deep furrow between his eyebrows. It never bodes well when Derek makes statements such as those. He never exaggerates; therefore, if he says he's bringing ill tidings, he's not lying.

"Go on. Drop the hammer," my uncle tells him.

"I received confirmation that the wolves from the Eriksson pack are preparing to meet with Larsson van Praag."

A rush of discontentment takes over the room. My mother makes a distressed sound in the back of her throat, which is the most audible noise around.

"What's wrong?" I ask.

"Nothing," she replies without making eye contact.

"Why are the dragons getting involved with other supernaturals?" I ask. "I thought they were content with living their reclusive lives."

"It's been a while since they decided to keep to themselves," Uncle Raphael replies. "It seems our war has renewed their taste for blood."

My face warms. That's new information to me, but it doesn't seem as if Lucca or Ronan are surprised.

What the hell? Why were they privy to that information and I wasn't?

"Why would he want an alliance with the wolves of all creatures?" my mother asks.

"I wasn't able to uncover that information before traveling here. All I know is Larsson sent a messenger to Melker's village, and that wolves are sending an envoy to meet the dragon king at the foot of the Indigo Mountain."

"No," Mom whispers.

"The Indigo Mountain? Are you sure?" Uncle Raphael asks.

Derek nods. "Yes. All three of my sources have confirmed the same."

"Do you think the Elder dragon has anything to do with it?" James Davenport, the leader of the Red Guard, asks.

Uncle Raphael rubs his face. "Given the location, and knowing Larsson, I can only assume as much. We cannot let this meeting take place without us."

"Are we going to show up uninvited?" Lucca asks, his eyes sparkling with excitement.

Unfortunately, I don't share his sentiment. I've never trusted dragons, and now I'm concerned about Karl. I don't know his place in the hierarchy of the pack, but what if he's part of the group traveling to the Indigo Mountain?

"Yes, I have to see it with my own eyes," Uncle Raphael replies.

"You can't possibly entertain that idea," Mom interjects. "After everything that's happened...."

Lucca twists his face into an expression of confusion, mirroring my own. Somehow, I don't think Mom is referring to the war.

"I can and I will. You won't make me change my mind, Natalia."

James shifts uncomfortably in his seat while the rest of us witness the intense staring contest between my mother and Uncle Raphael.

"And what if the wolves are indeed planning to ally with Larsson? What then?" I dare to ask.

"It'd be too much of a risk," Derek replies.

Uncle Raphael's gaze darkens. "Yes. There's no love lost between the vampires and the wolves. If they ally with the dragons, it won't be to our benefit. We can't allow that to happen."

My stomach twists into knots, and my throat becomes bone dry. "That means what exactly?"

I don't miss the meaningful glance my uncle shares with James.

"Why are you so interested in the fates of a pack of wolves, Manu?" Ronan asks in a tone of accusation, making me bristle in an instant.

"I'm not. Don't be ridiculous."

"I don't know yet what it means, Manu," Uncle Raphael answers my question. "But don't worry. We'll make sure no alliance is made between the dragons and the wolves."

His words are ominous, but it's the hint of danger shining in his eyes that puts fear into my heart.

I have to warn Karl somehow.

It's not easy to sneak out of my uncle's fortress when Ronan is keeping a watchful eye on me. I don't think he suspects what I intend to do; he's just hoping to corner me alone to have the talk.

Soon after Derek dropped the news about the possible meeting between the dragons and the wolves, Uncle Raphael dismissed everyone, save for Derek and James. Even my mother wasn't allowed to remain, which was surprising. Since my father passed away, Mom became more and more involved in warfare strategy, but it seems the subject of dragons is a source of conflict between her and my uncle.

After changing into clothes I stole from Lucca, I make sure my long hair is braided and out of the way, then pull the hood of my cloak over my head, satisfied that my features are mostly hidden. Only if someone gets into my personal space and has a closer look could they possibly know it's me. That's something Ronan would do, and for that reason, I decide to avoid the hallways altogether.

My chambers are four stories high, which makes jumping impossible. The fall wouldn't kill me, but my bones would shatter with the impact. Thinking that one day I'd need to escape my room this way, I fashioned a cord with old sheets and drapes a long time ago.

I tie one end to my bedpost since it's the heaviest and biggest piece of furniture here, then toss the other end out the window. The descent is child's play, especially without nonsensical skirts getting in the way. I land on soft feet and then wait a couple of beats, straining my ears to make sure there aren't any guards patrolling nearby.

My legs are tense, ready to break into a sprint toward the forest hugging the back of the castle. There's a high wall I need to clear beyond that, but the run between the castle and the forest is where I'll be most exposed.

Before I take off, I hear voices coming from the other side of the castle. It's Lucca and Ronan. The wind is blowing my way, so their conversation is clear enough, even though they aren't that close to me.

"Are you going to tell me why you were glaring at my sister during the entire meeting, or do I need to force it out of you?" Lucca asks.

"I wasn't glaring at Manu. Stop looking for problems where there are none."

"I wasn't born yesterday. Something happened between you two. Did you bed her?"

My spine goes rigid in an instant. *Will Ronan confess to Lucca?* I'm not ashamed, but that doesn't mean I want my brother to know.

"I did not," he replies calmly.

I can't believe he lied to his best friend without hesitation and so convincingly.

"Do you swear on your honor?"

Hell. I don't dare to breathe. If Ronan does swear, and then Lucca learns the truth, Ronan will lose another friend.

"I won't dignify such a ridiculous request. I'm telling you I didn't fuck Manu. That ought to be enough."

Nice evasion, Ronan.

Their voices are becoming fainter, which means they're not coming toward me. Regardless, I lingered too long. If I hope to make it to Karl's village tonight, I'd better go now.

Nine

KARL

ITALY, 1520

A week has passed since I helped the female vampire, and I couldn't stop thinking about her. Many times, I had to stop myself from venturing deep into the woods in the hopes of picking up her scent and finding out where she lives. One would think the urge would lessen as days went by, but my chest still aches with worry, and something else I can't decipher.

The meeting with the dragons will take place tomorrow night, which means the last week has been tense and unpleasant. Mom didn't miss any opportunity to recite her spiel that she believed it was a bad idea to meet with the fire-breathing beasts who could decimate our entire pack in one fell swoop.

The only person who benefited from her nagging was Cheryl. Our father stayed away from home for as long as he could, not coming in until he knew Mother was already retired. Thus, Cheryl's punishment was forgotten.

I'm about to head into the forest for an early evening run when I catch Cheryl trying to sneak in through the back door.

"What are you doing?" I whisper.

She jumps on the spot, placing a hand over her chest. "Curse you, Karl. You frightened me."

"I thought you were in your room, working on Father's new cloak."

"The cloak is sewn. I refuse to work on the ridiculous embroidery details until my fingers bleed. No one will see it when it gets caked in mud."

"I see. You do want an ass whooping, but from Mother, not Father." I smirk.

"Bite me, Karl. Where are you going?"

"For a run before the meeting with Father and the council."

She crosses her arms and pouts. "I hate that you get invited to those meetings and I don't just because I have a vagina."

"When I'm alpha, you'll have a chair next to mine. You have my word."

She snorts, clearly not mollified. "If you ever rise to that position."

"What do you mean?"

"Please. You know Dietrich wants it for himself. As soon as Father is gone, he's going to make a play for it and challenge you."

My spine becomes rigid as bitterness pools in my mouth. "And I'll be waiting for it. Don't worry, Cheryl, I'll never let Dietrich take what's rightfully mine."

She narrows her gaze. "If you mean that, then perhaps you should spend less time with that stupid flute of yours and more on the field with the rest of the wolves. Dietrich has been busy making his case that you're unfit to lead."

"How do you know that?"

She shrugs. "Sven can't keep a secret from me."

I pass a hand over my face. Did I suspect Dietrich was plotting something sinister? Yes. Did I lose any sleep over it? No, but perhaps I should have.

"And are the younger wolves buying his horseshit?"

Cheryl cocks her head to the side. "Oh, so you *do* care. I thought you were beyond pack politics."

"I don't care for it, but if Dietrich is spreading rumors about me, then that's of my interest. What else did Sven say?"

"I don't know, Karl. Why don't you ask him?"

I shake my head. "He might not be as open with me as he is with you."

"Why is that?"

"Come on, Cheryl. Don't tell me you don't know."

"Know what?" Her voice rises. "What are you insinuating, Karl?"

"He's completely infatuated with you."

Her eyes widen as if the idea is horrifying. "Sven is my friend. I don't think about him that way."

"Well, too bad, because he does, and he'll ask Father for your hand sooner rather than later." The blood seems to drain from her face, which surprises me. "You don't like that idea? He'll be a good match for you."

"I—"

"Cheryl?" my mother calls from inside the house.

"Rats. See what you did?"

"What did I do?" My eyebrows meet my hairline. "You ventured out without permission of your own volition."

"Yeah, yeah." She pushes the back door open and disappears inside the house faster than I can blink.

For her sake, I hope she has a good excuse if Mom does catch her sneaking in.

Instead of taking my clothes off by the tree line, I decide to do so here. No one is around to witness me, and Mom is busy with Cheryl at the moment. My skin breaks into goose bumps as soon as it meets the cold winter air, but I shift fast and break into a run.

As a wolf, I can still feel the winter's bite, but it's not unpleasant like it is when I'm in my human form. Cheryl hates the winter, but it's my favorite season despite the inconvenience. I love the feel of fresh snow under my paws and the crisp, cold air as it fills my lungs. Running in the forest is my coping mechanism when I'm overwhelmed and worried. I already had reason enough to need this run, but the conversation with Cheryl only served to give me more anxiety about the future.

I've always known Dietrich didn't like me, and he's too ambitious to allow me to rise to alpha peacefully, but I didn't believe the rest of the pack would listen to his poisonous words. I was naïve. I've been indulging too much in my other interests and forgot about a vital part of being a wolf: community. Not that I've been neglecting my duties as the alpha's son, but it seems I've acquired a bad reputation nonetheless, and that worries me. Sven wouldn't have mentioned anything to Cheryl otherwise. An alpha can't lead a pack if he doesn't have the respect of its members.

I lose track of how far I run, but tonight I can't linger in the forest or I'll be late for the meeting. I turn around and head back, hating that this short run wasn't enough to make me feel better. Even if I ran for hours, I'd still have this cloud of doom hanging over my head. Everything is happening too fast. There are too many life-altering decisions being made. An alliance with the dragons could change the tide for us, but the question is, would it change in our favor or against us?

My worrisome thoughts get shoved to the side when I suddenly pick up a familiar scent. *No, it can't be.* I slow down and try to pinpoint where it's coming from. The scent is not completely hers, it's mixed with something else, so it could be a figment of my imagination, or there's another vampire in the vicinity.

My heart speeds up as I search my surroundings. Then she steps in my line of vision, and I swear my heart stops beating for a moment. Her features are hidden, but I know it's her, the vampire female I saved, the one who's been occupying my head all this time. She's wearing leather pants and a tunic under her heavy cloak. It's clearly a male's clothing, judging by the size and the other scent I detected.

Immediately, a spike of jealousy takes over me, as I wonder if she's wearing the clothes of the warrior who came to her rescue. I don't dare move as I watch her approach me.

She pulls the hood back and says, "It's me."

Like I didn't know already.

But what is she doing here so close to our village?

"Can you shift? I really need you verbal for this conversation."

Yeah, so do I.

I shift even knowing I'll be freezing in no time. She doesn't speak for a couple of heartbeats as her eyes assess me. I don't have any issues with my nakedness, and it seems she doesn't either. However, my heart expands with pride when I notice her appreciation. She likes what she sees. That shouldn't animate my heart as much as it should put dread in it. She's a vampire, for heaven's sake.

"Why have you come? It's not safe for you here," I say.

She unclasps her cloak and offers it to me. "Here. I can't let you freeze to death on my account."

There's no chance I'll wear another male's cloak. Even in human form, my wolf is still influencing my decisions.

"I'm fine."

She furrows her eyebrows. "Is your male pride stronger than your survival instincts?"

I cross my arms. "I won't die. Trust me."

"Very well, then." She keeps the piece of clothing draped over her arm. "I heard you're planning to meet with the king of dragons."

Apprehension quickly takes hold of me. "How do you know?"

"My uncle has many spies. He's the king, after all."

My eyebrows shoot up. "You're King Raphael's niece?"

She nods. "I realize I never had the chance to formally introduce myself. My name is Manuela Della Morte, but you may call me Manu."

I force my expression into one of neutrality, but inside my head is another matter. It wasn't enough that I fell for a vampire's charms. She had to be royalty.

"I take it you've recovered, but still, why did you travel all the way here to tell me your uncle knows about our meeting? Is he planning to do something?"

Her gaze darkens. "Yes. He doesn't want an alliance between the wolves and the dragons."

"Why not?"

"Because it's not going to end well for us, and possibly for you as well."

I shake my head. "We're just trying to protect ourselves. You and your damn war is costing us lives. Several of our wolves were killed during the battle last week."

Her face crumbles, and her shoulders seem to curve forward. "I know. I'm sorry. But you have to understand, Larsson is not to be trusted. You're just getting in bed with a different kind of devil if you ally with him."

"And you just want me to take your word for it?"

My question has the bite of anger, though I'm not sure if I'm angry at her or about this whole situation. Manu's words are just a repeat of what my mother's been saying the entire week.

My sharp tone doesn't stop her from coming closer. "Yes. You must not attend the meeting at the foot of the Indigo Mountain. It won't end well for your pack."

"Is that a threat?" I snarl, and this time, she does react, her eyes widening.

"I'm not threatening you, damn it! I'm warning you. Please don't be foolish."

A low growl cuts off the retort that was on the tip of my tongue. I turn around and see Dietrich in wolf form, standing mere feet from where we are. Hell, I didn't even hear him approach. That's how much my argument with Manu distracted me.

The hairs on his neck are raised, and his lips are peeled back. He's a second away from attacking Manu.

I step in front of her, raising my arms. "It's okay, Dietrich. She's not the enemy."

He growls, maintaining his aggressive stance. Very few wolves would believe my statement. He would ignore me no matter what.

"I should go. I just wanted to warn you," she says.

I dare to glance away from Dietrich so I can get another glimpse of her face. But she's wearing her cloak again and has the hood up. I don't have a chance to say a word before she becomes a blur and vanishes into the dark forest.

Dietrich howls, reminding me that I still have to deal with him. I shift back into wolf form, but now that Manu is gone, he's no longer ready to pounce. Instead, he turns around and runs back to the village.

I don't need an oracle to tell me what he intends to do with that information.

I rush after him, hoping I can convince my father I'm not in cahoots with the enemy.

Ten

KARL

ITALY, 1520

I would have reached the village before Dietrich could spin a horrible story about me being a traitor if the bastard hadn't set a trap for me. I thought it was by chance that he found me with Manu, but now that I find myself surrounded by his followers, still deep in the woods where no one can come to my aid, I know he had been following me.

"What's the meaning of this?" I ask through the mind link all the wolves have.

"I knew you couldn't be trusted," Dietrich replies. *"I can't imagine the blow when Melker finds out his only son is in league with bloodsuckers."*

"I'm not in league with anyone," I snarl.

"Your lies will fall on deaf ears."

The channel connecting our minds shuts. Dietrick howls, and he's answered by the five wolves he's brought here. I prepare for the attack, but I once again underestimate his level of deceit. The whistle of an arrow cutting through air is the only warning I hear before I'm hit on my flank. The pain is sharp and draws a whimper from me.

Almost immediately, I begin to shift back into human form without meaning to do so. But it's the burning coming from the wound that tells me the tip of the arrow has been laced with wolfsbane.

Son of a bitch.

"You fucking coward," I grit out.

With the poison coursing through my veins, there's little I can do when members of Dietrich's posse tie me up and gag me. I struggle, but I'm too weak to cause any real harm to my captors. I'm tossed over someone's shoulder like a sack of dirty clothes and taken back to the village.

People have gathered when we reach the main square. It seems Dietrich has sent someone ahead to alert them of our arrival. Most carry torches, which grant their grim expressions an even more ghoulish appearance.

Dietrich's minion dumps me on the snow-covered ground, sending another bolt of pain from the arrow wound.

"What's the meaning of this?" my father asks, his voice echoing in the square.

"My suspicions were correct, Alpha. Your son has been colluding with those bloodsuckers," Dietrich replies, already back to his human form and into warm clothes.

I'm shivering, but all I can do is curl into a ball. My muscles are already turning irresponsive, either from the cold, the wolfs-bane, or both.

"Do you have proof of that?" my father asks.

"Yes, I saw him with my own eyes."

"I didn't betray the pack," I grit out.

Boots crunch on the snow, but I can only turn my head to see the scruff of worn leather. I don't need to look up to know it's my father who is standing next to me.

"Do you deny meeting with a vampire, Karl?"

"No. She came looking for me."

"Why would she do that if she wasn't your ally?" He crouches so he can better glower at me.

"She came to warn us that meeting with the dragon king is dangerous. That you shouldn't head to Indigo Mountain."

His face morphs into an expression of rage, and immediately I recognize my error. The punch to the mouth comes next, fast and sure, making it impossible for me to block it. Blood fills my mouth, but that's not the worst of it. It's the humiliation of it all.

"Bind him to the pole," my father orders.

I'm seized by rough hands and then dragged to the tall pole right in front of the great hall. The wolfsbane has put me completely at the mercy of my handlers, and they use that to their advantage, binding my hands above my head as tight as they can. My jaw is still throbbing from the punch. I lift my gaze and search for a friendly face in the crowd. I find none. When my eyes land on Sven, he turns the other way and leaves the square. *Coward.*

There's no sign of Cheryl or Mother. My sister wouldn't let this happen to me. She'd come to my defense even at the risk of getting the same punishment as me. Mother knows this. She must have prevented Cheryl from leaving the house.

When the first lash strikes my back, it catches me by surprise. I never knew it could burn so much. I don't know who is doling out my punishment, but I suspect it's Dietrich by the ferocity of the blows. I refuse to scream, even when it feels like I'll die from the next strike.

I try to detach not only from the physical pain of the whip lacerating my muscles but also from the pain of betrayal. I can't believe my own father wouldn't let me explain what truly happened in the forest. He was more than happy to take Dietrich's accusations at face value.

Manu's image comes to the forefront of my mind, and I latch on to it. The simple thought of her makes my soul lighter.

I don't know how long my punishment lasts, but she's the last thing I see before darkness claims me.

MANU

I'm almost at the invisible line that separates my uncle's territory from the forest patrolled by the wolves when a sharp tug in my chest makes me stop and turn around. Something is horribly wrong.

Karl.

His name pops in my head, and immediately I know he's in trouble. I never had the power to sense bad omens or foresee the future, but I know deep in my bones that his life is in danger.

That wolf who appeared in the forest, the one who wanted to tear me to shreds, he must have done something to Karl.

Without stopping to think what I'm doing, I break into a run, hoping I'm not too late to save him. The forest is a dangerous place for a lonely vampire. Not only wolves roam the area but also soldiers from Tatiana. The sense of urgency is telling me I don't have time to seek help. And who would I ask? Lucca would think I'm mad for worrying about a wolf, and Ronan... I don't know what he'd do, but he certainly wouldn't be inclined to assist.

I must do this alone.

I brought my sword, and I can hold my own against vampires, even if I'm outnumbered. Wolves are a different matter though. Their sharp teeth can do more damage than a sharp blade. I'm not wearing any armor, so if any of those shifters get a hold of my neck, I'm dead.

I banish those gruesome scenarios out of my head, keeping my senses sharp for any danger ahead as I cut through the silent forest at breakneck speed. I know I'm close to Karl's village when I smell blood spilled. My chest becomes tight.

I slow down and approach the edge of the forest more carefully. It's late, and the dwellings are shrouded in darkness; not a single torch illuminates the area. On soft feet, I brave out of the forest's coverage into the open. I pull my hood down because hiding my face is useless when a single whiff will tell the wolves what I am, and I can't have my peripheral vision blocked.

My stomach bottoms out when I get a visual of the square where the scent of blood is coming from. I suppress a gasp, horrified to see Karl bound to a pole, naked, his back ripped to shreds. There's also an arrow sticking from the side of his leg.

Fighting tears, I hurry to him and then drop to my knees.

"Karl," I whisper as I brush his hair off his face.

His eyes open to slits, but they seem unfocused. "Manu?"

"It's me. What have they done to you?"

"You shouldn't be here. If my father catches you, he'll kill you."

"Did he do this to you?"

He closes his eyes and nods.

Sudden fury erupts from the pit of my stomach. I want to find the son of a bitch and claw his heart out with my bare hands. But I can't do that when Karl is more dead than alive. I need to get him out of this damn village and find someone who can help him.

I jump back to my feet, and with a swipe of my hand, I cut him loose. He tumbles forward, almost colliding with the snow if I wasn't quick enough to prevent his fall. With him leaning against my shoulder, it's more difficult to unclasp my cloak, but I manage and then wrap it around him.

He hisses when the thick fabric covers his raw back.

"I'm sorry. I need to keep you warm. You're dangerously close to freezing to death. Can you stand?"

"No... the arrow. The tip was laced with wolfsbane."

My gums ache as my fangs descend. I can't help how my body reacts to my rage, but unfortunately, my thirst for revenge has nowhere to go, so I need to swallow it down for Karl's sake. I should remove the arrow, but it looks like it's been embedded in his skin for a while, and I might do more harm than good if I try.

"I'll carry you, then."

He doesn't protest when I lift him into my arms, even though I know it must be causing him excruciating pain to move.

"Maybe I should carry you over my shoulder."

"No. Please... this is fine."

I'd argue if we weren't moments away from discovery. I sweep the area to make sure we're still alone, then dash to the forest, not slowing down until I've put a good distance between us and that infernal village. But we're not free from danger yet. Karl's life is hanging by a thread, and I don't know how to help him. I can't take him back to my uncle's fortress, and I'm too far from any healer I know.

Desperation starts to claw its way up my throat, constricting my airways.

No, Manu. You can't let panic take control. Think.

Solomon Corvicus. The first familiar. He lives in a cottage on Uncle Raphael's territory, but not inside his walls. I've been there once, as a child, but the trip made a deep enough impact on me that I'm sure I can find the place again.

I glance at Karl before I resume my trek. He's unconscious, and his cheeks are as cold as ice despite the cloak around him. He's lost too much blood, and it isn't helping his case. If he was human, he'd be dead by now. I wish I could run faster, but falling with Karl in my arms could be disastrous.

"Please, Karl, hang on a little longer."

For me. For us.

Eleven

CHERYL

ITALY, 1520

My eyelids are heavy, and I can't open them right away. My brain feels like it's been scrambled, and as I try to remember where I am or what happened to me before I fell asleep, the memory slips from my grasp like ice. The heaviness in my heart tells me something awful happened though.

My body is leaden as I turn around, and my mouth tastes bitter. With effort, I open my eyes and realize I'm in my chambers. The knowledge doesn't give me comfort, not when the numbness assaulting me can only be attributed to one thing.

Wolfsbane.

I was poisoned.

Bits of memory trickle down, and with each piece of information I remember, my worry increases. Something happened to Karl, and Mother... she drugged me with wolfsbane to keep me from going after Father once he stormed out of the house.

Bracing my hands on the mattress, I push myself to a sitting position, and then toss my legs to the side of the bed. Wolfsbane is still in my body, and it won't completely be gone until morning. By then it might be too late to help Karl. I need the antidote.

Using the wall for support, I stagger to my feet. My legs shake with the strain of holding myself upright. *Goddammit, Mother. Why did you poison me?*

Locking my jaw tight, I force one leg forward but buckle and end up falling on my knees.

I guess crawling it is, then.

Even so, it's hard, and it takes me far too long to reach the other side of my room where I hid a stash of wolfsbane antidote. I didn't know what possessed me to do so. I did it on a whim about five years ago. Maybe it was a premonition that told me I'd need it one day.

I'm sweating when I reach the spot on the floor where I put the sash with the herbs I need. There's a loose piece of wood, and underneath is a small compartment where I hid the antidote and every piece of coin I could scrape together. My heart is drumming madly in my chest as I undo the cord keeping the sash closed. I hope the herbs are still edible. It's been so long. But even if they were moldy, I'd eat them.

Mercifully, I see no sign that a fungus is growing, but chewing on the dried plant almost makes me gag. I wish I had a pitcher of water handy. I swallow the bitter lump with difficulty, and then retrieve the rest of my treasure. It all fits in a small leather pouch that I tie around my leg. If I have to shift, I won't be forced to leave my coin behind.

The antidote works, and soon I recover the ability to move. I dress quickly and then press my ear against the door. The house is quiet, but that doesn't mean much. I don't know how late it is. It's possible that my parents have gone to bed.

When I try the door, I find it locked. I expected that. If Mother went through the trouble of drugging me, she really doesn't want me to escape my room. It was a vain effort on her part. I can jump out the window, as I have so many times before.

I push the shutters open, getting blasted by the cold air and something more alarming—blood mixed with the scent of pines. My heart shrivels inside my chest.

Karl.

Without looking back, I jump, landing in a crouch. Then I take off toward the square, where the scent of blood is coming from. When I reach the spot, I see the pole used for punishing wolves who misbehave. There's a circle of flesh blood surrounding it, and a cord that was recently cut by sharp claws, it seems.

I'm seized by rage and incredulity. There's no shadow of doubt that the wolf punished tonight was Karl. Tears gather in my eyes as I glance around the square with all its darkened buildings. They left him here to die, but somehow, he escaped.

I take a whiff of the cord and pick up another scent that isn't his. My muscles turn rigid. A vampire was here, but not any vampire. It's a smell I recognize. It was all over Karl when we got separated during the fight last week.

Did the vampire he fought come back to finish the job? I shake my head, denying the idea. There's no way a bloodsucker would be stupid enough to come into our village, only to finish off Karl. Besides, there isn't a splatter of blood consistent with a vampire attack.

I search the ground for clues and find one set of footprints moving away from the pole. Their size indicates a female vampire was here, but they make deeper indents in the snow. Vampires aren't ever overweight, which means she was carrying something heavy.

She took Karl with her.

I follow the footsteps, making sure I erase the trail as I go in case Father decides to come after us. I don't want anyone finding my clothes, so I won't shift until I'm deep in the woods. I'd run faster on four legs though. When I'm far enough away from the village, I shift, not bothering to get undressed first. My clothes rip during the process, but it isn't likely I'll return for them. No matter what happens, I can't come back to the pack.

I surrender my senses to the wolf and let it guide me to Karl. The forest becomes a blur as I run as fast as I can. If there's a trap in my path or the enemy, I won't see it until it's too late. But my concern for my brother is overriding everything, even my sense of self-preservation. Karl is the only one who understands me. He's my best friend. If something happens to him, I don't know what I'll do.

No, if he dies, there won't be a wolf left alive in that village. I'll destroy them all, starting with Dietrich.

The small hairs on my back stand on end when I detect several different vampire scents at once. I'm deep in bloodsucker territory now. They're making it hard to isolate Karl's kidnapper's scent. I slow down and take a deeper whiff of the cold air. Then I stop completely when I can't smell the bitch at all.

Hell, where did I lose her scent?

I'm about to retrace my steps when an arrow flies close to my ear. I whirl around and immediately see them, a group of three bloodsuckers. They've already spread out to make a circle around me. One of them carries a bow, and he's aiming another arrow at me.

I tense, ready to jump out of the weapon's path. There's no chance in hell I'll be stopped by these leeches. He fires and misses. His companions let out a war cry and unsheathe their swords. I'll deal with them later. The first vampire I need to dispatch is the one who can kill me at a distance.

Running in a zigzag pattern, I head his way. He freezes just before I pounce on him and sink my teeth into his arm. He's not wearing any armor, and his blood rushes into my mouth. It's not the most horrible thing I've swallowed, which surprises me.

"The wolf got Dean!" a male shouts.

I drag my prize away from the other two vampires, who are coming at me.

"Let me go!" The male tries to pull away, which makes me sink my teeth deeper.

He manages to hit the side of my head with such force that it makes me dizzy. It also enrages me more. I let go of his arm to aim for his jugular but stop short when I notice how young he is. He's probably no older than fifteen. It explains why instead of protecting his neck, he's busy cradling his arm.

The brief moment of distraction costs me. One of the vampires is within striking distance. He swings his sword and would have cut me in half if I hadn't managed to leap to the side. The heavy sword falls on a rock covered by snow, making the vampire curse either out of frustration or pain.

"Fucking hell," he shouts.

This one isn't a youngling, so I don't feel any qualms about taking a bite out of him. But unlike the first fool with the arrow, this male is wearing armor.

"Watch your back, Lucca," the third bloodsucker warns.

There goes my chance to jump on his back while he was distracted.

I dance away from his reach while trying to find an opening to escape. The third vampire is taller and bulkier than the first two, and by the way he holds his sword, I'd say he's more experienced too. But he can't block my path alone. When he charges, I wait until the last moment before jumping to the right. I miscalculate though, and the tip of his sword grazes my side. The cut burns more than it should, but I don't intend to let it slow me down.

Only I don't have a choice. My body is already shaking before my paws hit the snow, and then my legs give out from under me.

I let out a whimper as desperation sweeps over me. I'm shifting back to human, which means the vampire's sword was laced with wolfsbane.

Not this again.

Twelve

ITALY, 1520

"Is she dead?" Dean asks.

"No, I just nicked her." I walk over to the wolf who, thanks to the wolfsbane in my blade, has shifted back to human form.

Completely naked save for the leather pouch attached to her leg, she's curled up into a ball, and her shivering is obvious. She looks at me with hate in her green eyes. I'm struck by her appearance. Long ginger hair contrasts with the snow and her alabaster skin, and her full lips are bee stung and red. I've never seen a creature more lovely, and I can't look away.

"What are you looking at?" she snarls.

Lucca walks over and stands next to me. "Why have you come here, wolf?"

She ignores him, keeping her fiery eyes on my face. Her red lips are quickly turning blue, and icicles have already formed on her hair. I unhook my cloak and cover her with it.

"I don't need your pity," she tells me.

"Why are you helping her?" Dean asks. "She almost chewed my arm off."

"We can't interrogate her if she freezes to death," I reply.

I bend over and pick her up. Her body tenses, but she doesn't strike me or try to flee. She probably can't, thanks to the poison.

"You'd better leave me here to die. I'll never tell you anything."

"We'll see about that."

She grows quiet during the short trip back to King Raphael's fortress. The few soldiers we encounter at the gate stare at the female in my arms with a mix of curiosity and suspicion. Wolves never venture this close to our territory.

Sunrise is near; I can sense it in my bones. It was a chance of fate that Lucca, Dean, and I were in the forest this late.

More curious soldiers greet us once we're inside the fortress. The female seems to shrink into herself now that her chances of escaping have diminished to none. She's shaking, causing a twinge of remorse in me. All she did was cross into our territory. Dean attacked her first.

Nonsense, Ronan. Stop making excuses for the wolf shifter. With the meeting between them and the dragons happening tomorrow evening, her presence here is suspicious.

Natalia meets us in the main hallway, her purposeful walk meaning someone alerted her of our arrival.

"What happened?" She stares at Dean's wound, then at the female in my arms.

"We came across the wolf shifter in the forest, and Dean engaged," Lucca replies.

"Was I supposed to let her escape?" he retorts.

"No, but you should have waited until we were closer."

The young male doesn't like Lucca's criticism. He's not a bad kid, but he's too impulsive and eager to impress us. I understand his motivation. His father is the leader of the Red Guard, and he wants to make his old man proud. I don't blame him entirely for what happened in the forest. Both Lucca and I messed up too. If I hadn't laced my blade with wolfsbane, she would have escaped.

"You need to see a healer immediately," Natalia tells him, then turns to me. "What do you plan to do with her?" Her nostrils flare. "She's also been hurt."

"Just a scratch," I reply.

"Just a scratch, my ass," the female retorts.

"She lives." Lucca snorts. "I was beginning to think you had bit the dust."

"No, but I'll make sure you and your caveman friend do one day."

Natalia narrows her gaze. "She's feisty. You'd better pay extra attention to her."

"Where's Uncle?" Lucca asks.

"He's in a meeting with his generals. He probably wants to speak with the wolf when he's done."

"Of course." I nod.

"Now come, Dean. You're no use to the Red Guard if you lose your arm." Natalia steers the male down the hallway, and I turn in the opposite direction.

Instead of taking the stairs leading to the dungeons, I veer for the towers.

"Where are you going?" Lucca asks, trailing after me.

"I'm not taking her to the dungeons."

"Why not? It's where we take all our prisoners."

"It's too horrible down there."

My argument makes no sense, and clearly Lucca believes the same.

"She's a wolf," he replies exasperatedly.

"I already told you I don't need your pity, bloodsucker," the female replies, then has a coughing fit.

Lucca rolls his eyes. "Great. Don't tell me she's getting sick."

"If I'm getting sick, it's thanks to breathing the same air as you lot."

"Lucca, why don't you go find your sister and make sure she's not causing more trouble?" I tell him.

"Why? I want to know why that wolf was trying to breach the fortress."

I stop and give him a meaningful glance. "I think I'll be able to get more information from her on my own."

Lucca is a stubborn son of a bitch, but this time, he doesn't argue with me. Maybe it's the fact that we haven't seen Manu in hours, and she's prone to giving us a headache.

"Fine." Sulking, he retraces his steps.

"I can't believe he bought that lame excuse you gave him," the female says.

"It wasn't an excuse."

"Oh, so you really think you can get any information from me? You're delusional."

She's goading me, so I clamp my jaw shut and refuse to fall for it. Lucca's mother was right, this female is feisty, and it will be hard getting her to spill the truth. I don't think Lucca's presence would hinder my attempts, but I want time alone with her without witnesses. Lucca was distracted, but there's no doubt in my mind that he'd be able to sense my unusual interest in the female if he paid closer attention, and I don't want anyone to notice that.

The room I take her to is rarely used, though it does have a cot and a chair. I set her down and reach for the cloak. She growls at me.

"I just want to check your wound."

"You weren't worried about it a moment ago. What is it, bloodsucker? Do you have a thing for defenseless females?"

My eyebrows shoot up. "If you're implying that I want to take advantage of you, you're mistaken. I have honor."

She laughs without humor. "I saw your honor on the battle-field. Cutting down wolves for pure fun. You disgust me."

My nostrils flare. "We didn't kill anyone for sport. If there were casualties, it was in self-defense."

"You're full of shit."

I step away from her, forgetting her wound for the time being. If her tongue is still sharp, she's not on the verge of dying.

"Enough with the insults. Tell me what you're doing in our forest."

She smiles perversely. "No."

I unsheathe my sword. "Don't make me use this against you again."

Her eyebrows furrow. "Go ahead. Cut me into pieces. I dare you."

"Infuriating female." I yank the cloak off her, making her wince. She tries to cover herself, but she can't move her arms right.

I don't want to ogle her body, but my eyes have a will of their own. It's impossible to miss the milky color of her breasts or the rosy nipples that are hard as pebbles, thanks to the cold. I catch myself before my gaze travels south.

"I knew you were a perv." Her eyes fill with tears, and I can't tell if they're caused by fear or rage.

Either way, it makes me feel like a cad. I turn around and head for the window.

"Forgive me. I didn't mean to look. It was an involuntary reflex."

"If you're going to kill me, do it now. I'm not going to tell you anything."

"I'm not going to kill you." I look over my shoulder. "But King Raphael might."

"I'm not afraid of him either. I have nothing to lose."

Her lips quiver, and her pupils dilate.

Aha. The lie. She does have something to lose.

"You were looking for someone in the forest, weren't you?" I ask, risking the gamble.

Her eyes widen. "What do you know of my brother?"

Whoa. That was too easy. She must be truly desperate to find him, or she wouldn't have fallen for my trap.

"I know nothing of your brother. Why did you think you would find him here?"

She doesn't answer for a moment, and her eyes take on a calculating glint.

"I caught his scent. He was taken by one of you. A female vampire."

My spine becomes rigid in an instant. The wolf shifter I found with Manu last week had red hair, just like the female staring daggers at me. I can't believe I didn't notice the resemblance until now.

Hell, what have you done now, Manu?

"Your brother is not here."

I expect her to call me a liar, but instead, her face crumbles. She closes her eyes, and a small tear rolls down her cheek. A sense of protectiveness takes over me. I want to ease her agony, tell her we'll find her brother. But such sentiment is insane. She's a wolf shifter, and she'd probably rip out my throat with her sharp teeth if given the chance.

It's possible Manu took the male wolf, though for what purpose I don't know. I need to find her and make sure he isn't here.

"I'll return with clothes, food, and water."

"Why bother? It's not likely I'll leave this place alive anyway."

"You think we're soulless monsters, don't you?"

She opens her eyes and stares into mine. "Are you going to tell me you aren't?"

"We can be monsters to certain people, but I'm not yours."

Thirteen

MANU

ITALY, 1520

"**S**olomon! Open up. It's Manu Della Morte."

A light flickers inside, and then I hear the grumbles of the old male. He yanks the door open and glares at me over his large nose.

"What in the world?"

I push him out of my way and stride into the small house. The intense smell of moss, bark, and other herbs hits me at once, making my nose itch.

"I need your help."

"He's a wolf shifter," he mumbles. "You brought a wolf into my house. Are you daft, child?"

"I had no choice. He's been brutalized by his own pack and left out in the cold to die."

His bushy eyebrows furrow. "Wolves are savages, but they're also fiercely loyal. What did he do to earn such punishment?" He comes closer and looks under the cloak. "*Mamma mia.*"

"He helped me."

"Ah, that will do it. A wolf assisting a vampire...." He shakes his head. "No wonder they flayed him alive."

"He's lost a lot of blood. He was also shot by an arrow laced with wolfsbane. I fear he doesn't have much time left."

"You're right about that. Come on now. Set him on that bench, belly down."

I do as he says, careful not to hurt Karl further. Under the light from Solomon's torches, the visual is more gruesome than back in the village. I don't know how anyone can inflict that kind of punishment on a member of their community. Karl has done nothing wrong, save for exchanging a few words with me in the forest. Unless his pack found out he helped me during the battle last week. Regardless, this is all my fault, and the guilt pressing against my chest is relentless.

Solomon grabs several vials, pots, and herbs and begins to work. There's nothing for me to do besides stay out of the way and watch. I wring my hands together, trying to ignore the warning in my body that's telling me sunrise is not far away. But I can't leave this place before I know Karl will be all right.

Soon, the small dwelling is impregnated with a potent herbal smell. Solomon spreads a dark green salve on Karl's back, making him flinch.

"What's that?" I ask.

"A poultice that will help speed up his natural healing." He sets the pot aside and then examines the arrow wound in his leg. "You couldn't even remove the shaft?"

"I didn't dare risk it."

"Hmm, the wolfsbane-laced point has been embedded in his flesh for far too long. I'll need to brew a large quantity of the antidote."

He disappears down the corridor and doesn't return for a long while. I don't know exactly where he went, but I take the time alone with Karl to come closer. His skin is pale, and sweat has dotted his forehead.

With a sigh, I brush strands of his matted hair back. "I'm so sorry. This is all my fault."

I've never felt more anguish than I do now. Fighting back

tears, I lean down and kiss him softly on the lips. It's impulsive and reckless. I'm not quite sure what compels me to go against everything that's been ingrained in me. Vampires and shifters of any kind are an explosive combination. We shouldn't mingle, and yet I can't help it.

Karl stirs, and I jolt back. My heart jumps up to my throat, getting stuck there. A beat later, he opens his eyes and stares right into mine.

"Manu?" he asks in a raspy voice.

"Yeah, it's me."

"You came back for me?"

"Yes. I felt something was wrong and raced back. What have they done to you, Karl?"

He closes his eyes for a fleeting moment. "The alpha... my father.... It doesn't matter now."

"Was it because I came to warn you about the meeting with the dragons?"

"In part, but... other factors contributed to this outcome."

"Nothing justifies it. It's barbaric."

His brows furrow, but he doesn't have a chance to say whatever crossed his mind, for Solomon returns in that precise moment, carrying a mug of steamy brew.

"You're awake. Good. It will be easier if I don't have to force the antidote down your throat."

"Shouldn't you remove the arrowhead first?" I ask.

"His body is shutting down thanks to the poison. We need to address that before anything else."

"I didn't realize wolfsbane could be fatal. I thought it only slowed them down."

Solomon hands the mug to Karl, who only manages to drink a few sips before twisting his face in disgust.

"What foul concoction is this?" he growls.

"The antidote for wolfsbane," Solomon answers. "I had to brew it extra strong."

"I don't think I can keep it down if I drink more of it." He returns the mug to Solomon.

"Oh, quit being a baby. It's not that bad." He brings the brew up to his nose and makes a disgusted face. "Phew. It does smell foul."

Karl glares at him. "I dare you to drink it."

Solomon rolls his eyes. "Not in this lifetime, pup. I'm going to remove the arrow now. Brace yourself."

Karl's jawline becomes rigid as he stares into my eyes again. On instinct, I reach out and take his hand. He curls his fingers around mine and then turns to Solomon.

"I'm ready."

The familiar yanks the arrow fast in a precise move to cause the least amount of damage possible. But the tip is serrated and meant to tear the muscle as it's removed. Karl grunts and squeezes my hand tighter. His eyes are squeezed shut, and it seems to me he's looking more gray than white. I wish I could take his pain away, but all I can do is hold on to him.

Dark blood oozes from the wound. The smell isn't right. It's rancid, as if the blood has gone bad. Solomon uses a clean rag to contain the flow. I fear Karl is going to bleed to death, but eventually the blood coming out of the wound smells cleaner and then stops spewing out in rivulets.

Solomon applies the same greenish balm to the gash as he did to Karl's back, then stitches him up. Karl doesn't make a sound and keeps his eyes closed. I'm not sure if he's passed out or not. Every time Solomon inserts the needle into his flesh, he flinches ever so slightly.

After the sewing job is done, Solomon bandages Karl up and declares, "All done."

"Thank you," he replies feebly.

His hand is still clasped in mine, but the hold is slacking.

Solomon turns to me. "You need to go, Manu, unless you want to spend the day cooped up here. I don't recommend it.

Furthermore, I don't need Ronan and Lucca kicking my door down like the hooligans they are."

Part of me wishes to stay, but Solomon is right. If I don't return to the fortress before sunrise, there will be hell to pay. I do not wish to explain to my uncle that I missed curfew because I was by a wolf's bedside.

"Is he going to be okay?" I ask.

Karl opens his eyes. "Go. Please don't get in trouble because of me. I already feel much better."

I narrow my eyes, trying to fish out the lie in his statement. I also don't move or let go of his hand.

"He's not going to die," Solomon assures me. "At least not from his wounds. If you stay here and your brother or Ronan catches you with him, that's another story."

"Okay, I'm going," I tell him, then turn to Karl. "I'll be back to check on you after sunset."

"Tomorrow is the meeting with the dragons," Karl says.

"Don't tell me you still care about their fate after what they've done to you?"

Karl looks away. "I don't know what I'm feeling."

"Manu...," Solomon warns me. "Go now or don't. Your window is diminishing."

Karl releases my hand. "Go home, Manu."

I look him in the eye. "I'll be back."

As I turn, I catch Solomon's disapproving glance. I know he believes my actions are wrong, but I'm not going to abandon Karl after I brought so much pain to him.

The moment I step outside, my entire body goes rigid. The small hairs on the back of my neck stand on end as the primordial instinct to seek cover takes hold of me. The sky is already turning pink, which means I'll have to fly like the wind to avoid turning to ashes.

I take off, and my mind zeroes in on one thing only—getting to safety. My worry for Karl takes a step back. I don't slow down, not even when I cross the first gate. The grand doors to the main building should all be locked already, but there's a secret passage only the royal family and the inner circle know about. Unfortunately, it means a longer period outside, and I can feel the first rays of sun rushing toward me.

Finally, I see the shrubbery that hides the entrance. I dive between them and then dash down the stone steps just as light licks my back, burning at once. Mercifully, the secret door is under an alcove. I hide in the shadows and then pull the skeleton key I carry around my neck from under my tunic. My hand is shaking as I unlock the door.

Once safely inside, I let out a breath of relief. *That was close.*

My sentiment is short lived though. Lucca steps into the light cast by the torches, blocking my way.

"Where the hell have you been?"

I press my hand against my chest, a futile attempt to try to slow my heartbeat down.

"With Solomon."

He leans closer and takes a whiff of my neck. "You reek of wolf. I think it's high time you tell me what's going on, Manu."

I swallow the lump in my throat. I wanted to keep Karl a secret for as long as I could, but I can't bullshit my way out of this conversation. Lucca is my dear brother, and I used to tell him everything until the whole mess with Ronan, and now this.

I let out a resigned breath. "Very well. I'll tell you. But not here. Come to my chambers."

We walk in silence down the corridor. The only sounds echoing against the stone walls are our footsteps. When I enter my chambers, I make a beeline for the fireplace. Now that my heartbeat has decreased, I can feel the cold.

"You got burned," Lucca says.

"A little. It's already healing."

"Why did you wait so long to return to the fortress? What kept you in Solomon's shack until moments before sunrise?"

I'm not sure how Lucca will react when I tell him the truth, so I keep my gaze on the fire.

"I had to help a friend."

"A wolf friend?" There's no reproach in his tone, just curiosity.

"Yeah. He helped me during the confrontation last week."

Lucca stops next to me and stares at the fireplace as well. "You never told me what happened, and Ronan was also tight lipped about it."

"Because of the wolf," I say.

It's not a lie, but it's not the whole truth either. Maybe I should tell Lucca the whole thing and be done with it, but as I open my mouth to confess, I can't find the words.

"Right. So what happened to him, then?" Lucca asks.

"How do you know I'm referring to a male?"

"Manu, please. I can tell the difference between female and male scents. Don't evade the question. What happened to your friend?"

"I sought him out to warn him about the danger of his pack meeting with Larsson. I owed him that much. But a member of his pack saw us together. Karl was punished for his association with me."

"Wolves are savages."

"They aren't that much different than us. Betrayal is also punished by death among vampires."

He scoffs. "But at least we have a trial. I bet your friend didn't. What did they do to him?"

"They whipped him until his back was nothing but torn muscle, poisoned him with wolfsbane, and left him outside to die. When I found him tied to the pole, he was barely alive."

"You ventured into the wolves' village?" Lucca's voice rises an octave. "Are you crazy, Manu? If they caught you there—"

"They'd tear me to pieces. I know. I couldn't let Karl die though. So I freed him and took him to Solomon."

Lucca rubs his face. "Is he okay?"

"Yeah."

We don't speak for several beats.

"We'll have to tell Uncle about this," Lucca says what I dreaded he would.

"Why? You know what he'll do to Karl."

"He's not going to kill the wolf, Manu."

"How do you know that?"

"Karl doesn't have a pack anymore, which means there's no sense of loyalty keeping him from telling us what his former alpha plans to do with the dragons. Right now, Karl is an asset."

My heart shrivels into itself as I look at him. "So you want to use him as an informant? And then what happens when he tells us everything?"

He meets my gaze. "You care about him, don't you?"

I attempt to hide the nature of my true feelings, but it's pointless. Lucca knows me too well.

I look away. "It doesn't matter what I feel. He's a wolf, and I'm a vampire. The very idea of us is impossible."

"Not impossible, but it will very likely end up in tragedy."

I glower at him. "Thanks a lot."

He shrugs. "I only speak the truth."

"I don't understand this feeling swirling in my chest, Luc. I know it sounds insane, but whenever I think about never seeing Karl again, it brings me such sadness that I don't think I can bear it."

"Is your connection to the wolf that strong?"

"Yes."

Lucca crosses his arms over his chest. "It just occurred to me that you don't have a familiar yet, Manu."

"What are you saying?"

He smirks. "I'm saying you're wrong. The idea of a wolf and a vampire is not an impossibility, it's just a matter of perspective. Wolf shifters are part animal, aren't they?"

I shake my head. "Yes, but... can you please not tell Uncle yet? Or anyone else?"

"Manu... you know I can't do that."

I reach for his hand. "Please, Lucca. Give me one more day. You can tell Uncle tomorrow."

The deep *V* his eyebrows form makes me fear he won't grant me the favor, but then his expression softens.

"Very well, Manu. I'll wait until tomorrow."

Fourteen

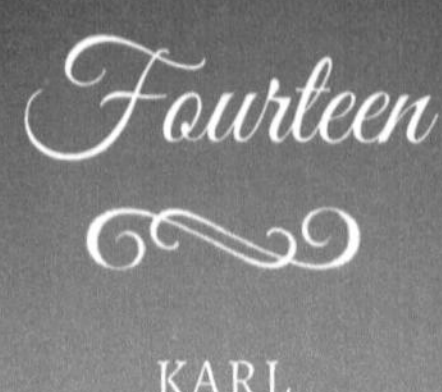

KARL

ITALY, 1520

I wake up covered in sweat, but the ache from the lashings has diminished considerably. At first, I don't know where I am, but then the faint smell of Manu's scent reaches my nose, and the last memory I had over her fills my mind.

She found me in the forest and brought me to Solomon Corvicus, the first familiar. There are blank spots in my memory, but one vivid image remains.

She kissed me.

I'm lying on my belly on a hard surface, covered in some kind of animal pelt. Bracing my hands against it, I push myself up. Too fast though. The movement sends a ripple of pain across my back. I guess I'm not completely recovered after all.

"What are you doing?" Solomon asks from the arched entryway. "You're not supposed to move until you're healed or you'll have horrible scars."

"I don't care. Where's Manu?"

Solomon's bushy eyebrows meet his hairline. "Ah, that's the source of your agitation. She left a while ago, you know, on account of the sun coming up. You don't remember?"

"No. There are a lot of details missing from my memory."

He rubs his chin. "Hmm, must have been the painkiller I added to the wolfsbane antidote."

"How long have I been here?" I ask, noticing the roughness in my voice.

I don't remember screaming while I received my punishment, but maybe I did afterward.

"Let's see. Manu brought you in the middle of the night, and it's now almost sunset."

I've been gone for too long. Surely Cheryl must be distressed with worry. She wasn't present during my punishment, but I'm sure by now she must have learned of it. I need to make sure she's okay. I hope she didn't do something stupid and get herself the same fate I did.

I pass a hand over my face, letting out a shaky breath.

"I have to return to my village."

Solomon's eyes widen. "You can't be serious. After they flayed you alive?"

"My sister is there. She's not safe."

He shakes his head and mutters something unintelligible under his breath.

"What was that?" I ask.

"Just wondering how I let myself get embroiled in the affairs of every supernatural creature in the land, like I didn't already have my hands full with the bloodsuckers."

I stand up, wincing in the process. I'm naked save for the bandages covering my back. "I need clothes. I don't think I can shift yet."

He puts his hands on his hips and glares at me from his lower height. "Do I look like a tailor to you?"

"Of course not. I'll take anything, even an old blanket."

"Don't be dense. In your condition, you'll freeze before you reach your village. In case you forgot, we're in the middle of winter."

A growl escapes my throat. "I need to check on my sister."

Solomon narrows his eyes. "What you need is to calm the fuck down. What if I told you there is a way to see if your sister is all right without leaving my humble premises?"

I arch my eyebrows. "Are you talking about using magic?"

He nods.

"I didn't know familiars could wield it."

"Well, they can't, but I'm not just any familiar."

Right, he's the first, and the only one not bound to a vampire.

I nod. "If there's a way, then show me."

I watch the small creature walk to a cupboard filled to the brim with tomes and scrolls. He opens a drawer and pulls out a small, round object. The way he holds it, almost reverently, tells me he considers it a treasure.

"What's that?"

He walks over, clutching the object against his chest. "This is a relic that belongs to a very powerful being. You may never tell anyone I have it."

My eyes widen. "Did you steal it?"

He narrows his eyes. "No, I borrowed it."

Borrowed, my ass. I keep the comment to myself though.

"I won't tell anyone. You have my word."

He snorts. "Like I'll rely on anyone's word."

"Then why—"

He throws a powder in my face that ends up in my mouth, giving me a coughing fit.

"*Mum est verbum,*" he recites.

My tongue tingles as magic sweeps into my mouth and down my throat.

What the hell?

"What have you done to me?" I choke out.

"Making sure you keep my secret. Now, look into the mirror and think about who you want to see."

I've heard of mirrors before. They're made from polished metal that shows someone's reflection when you stare at it, like the surface of a river. But this one is different. Its surface is made of glass that reflects my face with perfection. It's clearer than when I look at the most crystalline lake.

"Who did this belong to?" I ask.

"It's best if you don't know."

"What material makes this?" I run my fingers over it.

"Don't know. It's Nightingale-made."

"Nightingale?" My voice rises.

The Nightingales are the powerful immortals who created the vampires. I almost drop the object on the floor as if it burned my skin. Those creatures are considered anathema among wolves.

Solomon curses under his breath. "Blast my big mouth. You'd better forget I said anything, boy."

"I'm not a boy. Besides, didn't you put a spell on me so I wouldn't talk?"

"I did. But if by ill fortune you're captured by folks initiated in witchcraft, my spell might not be enough."

"Fantastic," I grumble.

"Too late now. The cat is out of the bag. Go on, retrieve the information you seek or give my mirror back."

What a prick.

I try to maintain my glare, but my eyes drop to the object offered. I do want to know if Cheryl is okay, so I focus on my reflection and think about her. When I curl my fingers around the handle of the small mirror, a rush of ancient power flows into me. I've never felt anything like it in my entire life. It's no wonder my kind is leery of the Nightingales. The power is neither good nor evil, but it doesn't feel good as it courses through me.

At first, all I see is my reflection, but then the surface ripples just like the waters of a lake when it's disturbed. Immediately, I begin to feel light headed and lose the sensation of my body. My instincts are screaming in my head to let go of the mirror, but it's almost like I physically can't do it. Instead, I find myself leaning closer until it feels like I'm plunging into it.

Total darkness consumes me, and I begin to panic. Then

finally, I see Cheryl. She's in her room, sleeping. A wave of relief washes over me. She's safe.

Her image fades, and then another scene appears before me, but it's nowhere familiar. A room much larger than my parents' living room with walls made from polished dark stone is what I see. A fire blazes, bathing everything in orange, including the dark-haired beauty walking in front of it.

Manu Della Morte. I'm in her chambers.

Why did the mirror bring me here and not show me Cheryl instead?

I'm pulled back suddenly, and then the object is yanked from my hand.

"You shouldn't have done that," Solomon grits out.

"Done what?" I press a hand against my forehead, hoping the gesture will make the room stop spinning.

"Gone to see her. What were you thinking?"

"The mirror took me there. Wait. You know where I went? Did you see it too?"

He narrows his gaze. "I didn't need to see it. I felt the change in you."

My heart is beating much faster now. Is that the change he's referring to?

"What change?"

He throws his hands up in the air. "I'm with stupid. That's the only explanation. I swear this will become the butt of a joke one day."

"You may have saved my life, but I will not stand here and listen to your insults."

He cocks his head at me. "Hmm, maybe you don't know. How could you? That's not something that has ever happened before."

"What are you saying?"

"It seems, my dear wolf boy, you're mated to a vampire princess."

I feel the blood drain from my face. I stagger back and brace against the wall to avoid falling to the floor.

"Impossible," I whisper. "Wolves can only mate among themselves."

He shrugs. "I know what I felt."

I shake my head while denial bounces around in my mind. *This can't be.*

"That presents a very serious problem," he continues.

"I don't have to worry about my pack anymore. They've already cast me out as a traitor."

"I'm not talking about your pack, boy. King Raphael is the one to worry about. With the imminent alliance between the wolves and the dragons, I wouldn't put it past him to break you into pieces with his bare hands."

"I'm not afraid of him."

In truth, I'm not, but I know Solomon speaks the truth. I must have a death wish.

"Sadly, I know you're not."

"I need to go see Manu."

Pinching the bridge of his nose, he groans. "You didn't listen to a word I said, did you? If you're caught near King Raphael's fortress, you're dead."

"I won't get caught," I reply with confidence.

"Oh really? And how are you going to accomplish that?"

"You're going to help me."

He twists his face into a scowl. "And why would I do that?"

"Because if you don't, I'll find a way to remove your gag spell, and I'll tell anyone who cares to listen what you have in your possession."

He watches me through slits. "You wouldn't dare."

"Do you want to gamble?"

"That's the thanks I receive for saving your life?"

"If you help me sneak into King Raphael's fortress, you'll have my loyalty forever."

He scoffs. "What good is that to me, wolf boy? You'll be dead in a few decades."

"Then you'll have my loyalty for as long as I live."

He shakes his head, but he's no longer glowering, so that gives me hope.

"Fine. But if you get caught, you'd better not say I helped you. I don't need to suffer the wrath of the king."

I nod. "You have my word."

MANU

I've been pacing nonstop inside my room, counting the hours until sundown. Forget sleeping. I'm too worried for that. Leaving Karl's side was one of the hardest things I've had to do in my life. I touch my lips, remembering the kiss I stole from him while he was unconscious. I can't believe my boldness. He's a wolf shifter, the son of the alpha. We don't belong together.

My heart rebels against the idea of never seeing him again though. Why does he beguile me so much? Why do I want to risk my uncle's rage for only another moment with him? Even if he wasn't a wolf, he's a stranger.

The conversation with Lucca comes to the forefront of my mind again. I don't want to entertain the idea that Karl could potentially become my familiar. For starters, I don't know if that's possible. Familiars are animals that choose to become bound to vampires. Karl is not an animal. He has a human form too. Besides, my feelings might be one sided.

A gust of chilly air licks the back of my neck. I pivot swiftly, already on high alert. There shouldn't be any drafts coming from that direction. My ears detect a barely audible thud, as if someone landed on soft feet nearby.

Hell. There's an intruder in my room.

With my heart stuck in my throat, I pick up the closest weapon to me, the firepit poker, and tiptoe toward the noise.

I lift my makeshift weapon, ready to strike, when Karl steps from the shadows with his hands raised.

"It's me."

A wave of relief washes over me as I lower the poker, but my breathing is still coming out in bursts. "What are you doing here? How did you get in?"

"I'm sorry if I frightened you. It wasn't my intention."

I should be raving mad that he scared me like this, but I'm more worried than angry. The last time I saw him, his back was raw from all the whiplashes he received from his father, and he could barely hold on to consciousness.

"Did something happen?" I take a step forward but stop before I do something foolish like kiss him again.

It was one thing for me to steal a kiss from him while he wasn't awake. Quite different to do so now and risk him rejecting me.

"I had to see you." He moves forward, stopping short of invading my personal space.

He's so close to me now that I can smell the salve Solomon applied to his back, mixed with his natural wolf scent.

"Why?" I ask through the lump in my throat. I've never been this nervous before in the presence of a male, not even when I gave my virginity to Ronan.

"To thank you for saving me."

"I.... You didn't need to risk your life to do that. If anyone sees you here, it won't end well."

He lifts his hand and cups my face. His palm is warm and rough, and it sends zings of excitement down my spine. His intense green gaze collides with mine, and I feel myself falling into the depths of his eyes. My lips part when his thumb caresses my flushed skin.

"I wouldn't have a life if it weren't for you." His arm snakes around my waist as he steps forward.

There's barely any space left between our bodies. My chest is heaving, and my nipples become as hard as pebbles, straining against the fabric of my chemise, which I just remember is see-through.

But his eyes don't stray from my face. It's almost like he's drinking me in, committing my image to memory. A wave of desire rushes through me at the same time warmth spreads through my chest. I never wanted anyone to kiss me as much as I want him to do it.

"Karl...."

He leans down and places a soft kiss on the corner of my mouth. His touch makes me tremble, and my knees go weak. I close my eyes, surrendering to the sensation.

"Is this okay, Princess?" he asks in a rough voice.

"Yes," I hiss.

He slides his hand from my cheek to the back of my head and wraps his fingers around my unbound hair. I look at him again and see his eyes have turned wolfish. The sparks of desire have also ignited a different hunger in me. I'm craving not only his body but his blood.

Will he let me drink from him, or will he be disgusted by it?

He pushes my doubts to a dark corner in my mind when he slants his mouth over mine, searing me with his burning kiss. Holding on to his arms, I surrender to him wholeheartedly, melting into him. His tongue tastes like winter and fire, like stars in a moonless sky. He makes me dizzy and light. I'm a feather floating on air, waiting for the next breeze to send me soaring high.

He pulls back much too soon, and I want to weep.

"I haven't been able to erase you from my mind, Princess," he whispers against my lips.

"Nor have I, Karl. Are we crazy for feeling this way?"

"If we are, I don't want to be sane."

He kisses me again, deeper, rougher, and I love every moment of it. He releases my hair and runs his hand down my spine until he reaches the curve of my ass. My hands go on an exploration of their own, but I'm careful when I slide the tips of my fingers down his back.

"Does this hurt?" I ask.

"No. The skin is still tender, but your touch is a soothing balm."

I step away from his embrace and take in his entire frame. He's wearing peculiar clothing, a shirt that doesn't seem like it was made from cloth. I can't help but frown a little at his ensemble.

"Where did you get those clothes?"

He looks down and then back at me again from under ridiculously long eyelashes. His lips curl into a grin. "Solomon had to magically put this together using whatever he had in his dwelling."

"Take it off."

His eyebrows arch, and then his lips split into a broad smile. "You like seeing me naked, don't you?"

"Yes."

Without taking his eyes from me, he unclasps his cloak and lets it fall in a heap by his feet. Then he unlaces the top of his tunic and pulls it over his head. My mouth becomes dry as I imagine running my tongue over the hard ridges of his chest and abs. I get lost in my wild imagination, and when I return to the here and now, Karl's pants are also gone.

My eyes travel down, locking on the proof of his desire. I can say without a shred of doubt that I'm about to burst into flames. I force my gaze back to his face, and now his eyes are glowing yellow. My hands are shaking as I reach for my chemise laces. Slowly, I untie them and then let the soft fabric cascade down my shoulders.

His eyes glow brighter as his gaze sweeps over my body. It's a phantom caress that's wreaking havoc in my mind. I'm about to lose control, and I don't know if he's ready to see it.

We don't move for a couple of beats, and then something

within me snaps. We both move at the same time, crashing together in the middle of the room in a vortex of tongues, teeth, and hands. Concerned about my savage vampire nature, I forgot Karl is a wolf, and his beast sings to my monster. I jump into his arms, wrapping my legs around his hips. His erection presses against my belly, hard and promising.

My fangs are on display, and in the frenzy of the moment, I nick his lower lip. The instant his blood touches my tongue, it's over. A violent orgasm hits me out of nowhere, making me relinquish any grasp I had on my self-control. I want to bite his neck, drink more of his addictive nectar, but all I do is moan against his lips.

Karl leans back and asks me where the bed is. He knows what just happened to me. Unable to speak, I point with a shaky finger.

He strides toward it as he captures my mouth again. Even distracted, he manages to get us there without colliding with any wall. His body is shaking with urgency, just like mine is, yet he places me on the mattress with care and then sits at the edge.

"What?" I ask when he doesn't make a motion to join me.

"You're breathtaking. I thought as much the first time I saw you."

"I was wearing armor. Hardly an attractive ensemble."

"There's nothing more alluring than a beautiful female warrior." He smiles, showing me dimples that give him a boyish look.

My heart lurches forward and then constricts painfully in the next breath. I'm torn between savoring the moment and worrying that this could be the only time we spend together.

I stretch out my arm and touch his chin. "You're too far from me. I need you closer, much closer."

He begins to lean forward, then stops abruptly, his eyebrows in a deep *V*.

"What's wrong?" I ask.

"I can't go on without telling you something first."

My stomach twists painfully as my head begins to conjure up the most horrible scenarios.

"Very well."

"There's a chance... at least Solomon believes it to be true...." He runs his hands through his long hair.

"What is it? Whatever it is, we can sort it out together."

"There's a chance you're my mate."

My blood, which was pumping with desire a moment ago, seems to freeze in my veins.

"That can't be possible. I'm a vampire."

His face grows even more serious. "I know. I can't ignore Solomon's words though. This feeling swirling in my chest is strong and possibly the most wonderful emotion I've ever felt for anyone."

My heart speeds up, running at breakneck speed. My ears buzz with the sound of my pulse drumming in them.

"Does that mean what we feel for each other isn't real?"

"No, it's real. Too real."

"Too real?" I quirk an eyebrow.

He shakes his head. "I misspoke. Fated mates are not something common among wolves. It only happens on the rarest occasions and most often out of great necessity."

"Are you saying that if you're my mate, it's because the world needs us to be together?"

"Something like that."

My yearning for him doesn't diminish with the revelation, but it becomes less precious to me.

"If magic is at work, how can we trust our feelings?"

"You can't separate them. Once the mating bond sets, it becomes our reality. Our feelings are truer than anything."

A huge lump lodges itself in my throat. I can't wrap my mind around such a concept, but I also don't want to let him go.

Perhaps reading my silence as a refusal, he begins to stand.

I grab his wrist. "Where are you going?"

"I understand if you never want to see me again."

"I don't want you to leave. Please, stay."

I tug him toward me, and this time, he comes all the way. His lips don't cover mine though. He buries his face in the crook of my neck and licks my skin until his teeth find my earlobe. Letting out a needy moan, I arch my back. He releases my ear to trail open kisses over my chin, down the column of my neck until he reaches the curve of my breast.

I suck in a breath, shivering in anticipation, and wait for what he's going to do next. He peers at me with eyes gleaming with desire. His lips are parted, allowing me to see the hint of his fangs.

"If you're my mate, I want you to mark me as such," I say.

His brows arch. "Do you want me to bite you?"

"Yes," I reply breathlessly.

He doesn't answer for a couple beats, and I fear I said the wrong thing. *What if wolves don't bite each other during lovemaking? What if he realizes I'm a freak?*

"Only if you bite me too."

I gasp. "Do you mean that?"

"I want you to drink from me, but I won't drink from you though. That's not something wolves do. I hope that's okay."

Heavens, he looks so sheepishly adorable that I'm torn between pulling him into a hug and turning him around so I can ride him until we both forget who we are.

But Karl doesn't give me the chance to do either of these things. He dives for my breast and sucks my nipple into his mouth while his hand plays with the other. He bites me softly, then licks the spot with his tongue. I rub my thighs together, already delirious with desire. I wish his body was covering mine; I want to feel the weight of him over me, and the strength of his cock between my legs.

"Karl, please," I moan.

"What do you want, Princess?"

I capture his face between my hands and tug him upward. He slides his body over mine, positioning himself where I so desperately need him to be. I kiss him deeply, careful not to nick his lips this time. I don't want a small sample of his blood. I want to drown in it.

Karl grinds his hips against mine, simulating what's to come. I part my legs and moan immediately after when his length presses over my bundle of nerves. I'm slick with arousal and so ready for him that one tiny movement of my hips has him sheathing himself in me.

"Fuck," he groans against my lips.

My eyes roll back in their sockets as another orgasm approaches. I lift my knees and hook my legs at the ankles behind his ass. He takes that as a sign and plunges into me fast and hard. I kiss him on his neck, then tease the skin with the tips of my fangs. Karl groans louder.

"Do it, love. Drink from me." He offers me his neck, and I get tunnel vision. All I can see is his vein, pumping the most delectable nectar.

I sink my teeth into his flesh, and the blood rushes into my mouth. Karl moves faster, growing larger inside me. My body shatters as I drink his blood, and not much later, he screams my name as he empties himself in me.

I've never drunk wolf blood before, and now I don't think I can ever consume anything else.

Fifteen

RONAN

ITALY, 1520

I'm on my way back to the room in the tower when I cross paths with Lucca.

"Did you find Manu?" I ask him.

He stops short, almost as if I startled him with my question. He seems distracted or he would have sensed my presence in the hallway before he got a visual of me.

"Manu, ah yes. She's in her chambers."

"What's with the face? Did she do something?"

He shakes his head, almost in a daze. "No. She's fine. Don't worry about her."

"Good. One less thing to worry about."

Lucca drops his gaze to the items I'm carrying. "Are you bringing the wolf clothes, food, and drinks?"

"She's our prisoner, but that doesn't mean we ought to make her suffer. We're not savages."

He holds his hands up. "Whoa. Relax. I'm not criticizing you, just making an observation."

"I'm sorry. I think finding the wolf in the forest and the

approaching meeting between the wolves and dragons has set me on edge."

"We're all on edge. Did you gain any information from her?"

"Yes. She was looking for her brother."

Lucca's demeanor changes in an instant. His spine goes rigid, and his eyes grow larger. "What makes her think she'd find him in our territory?"

"She tracked him here."

He stretches his arms. "Hand over those items."

Suspicion takes hold of me. I narrow my eyes and watch him closely now. "Why?"

"Trust me, Ronan. I need to speak with her alone. You'll understand my reason soon enough."

I'm reluctant to agree with Lucca's idea, but the reality is he outranks me. If he truly wants to interrogate the female wolf by himself, there's nothing I can do. Pushing the issue might make him wonder why I want to be with her alone. To be honest, I don't know the answer to that question. Perhaps it's better if Lucca speaks with her this time.

"Very well. Good luck. She's trapped, but she's not tamed."

"Don't worry. I know how to handle difficult females. I've had plenty of practice with Manu."

CHERYL

It was foolish of me to reveal to the blond vampire that I was looking for Karl. He caught me by surprise when he asked me the right question. I understand now it was a gamble on his part, and I fell for it. I have no reason to believe he lied about Karl's whereabouts. I know he's not in this castle; I'd already lost his scent when I stumbled upon the vampires.

But just because I was weak once in his presence doesn't mean I have to continue being so. As a matter of fact, I should use that to my advantage. He thinks I'm broken, that I've given up. Maybe I did for a brief moment, but the fight has not left me yet. Karl might not be in this fortress, but he's somewhere nearby, and he needs my help.

The wolfsbane is finally beginning to weaken its hold on me. I can move my body, albeit still a bit sluggish, but I don't want to show my hand yet. Let the towering vampire think I'm still a helpless prisoner.

When I hear footsteps approaching my prison cell, it's hard to keep my body prone and not use my arms to cover myself. Wolves don't have issues with nudity, and we don't stare at each other. I saw the way the bloodsucker reacted to my nakedness. His eyes lit up with male appreciation, even if he didn't mean to do it.

The door opens, but it's not the blond vampire who comes to pay me a visit this time. It's his companion, the dark-haired male. He brought the items his friend promised me. Unlike him, he doesn't seem to give a fuck that I'm naked. His dark eyes remain glued to my face.

"I brought you clothes. Are you able to dress by yourself, or do you need assistance?"

"I can manage on my own."

He walks over to my cot and drapes a blanket over me. When his friend left the room, he took his damn cloak with him, leaving me exposed to the cold room.

"Then you might prefer to do it when I'm not here."

"Where's your friend?" I ask.

"I told him to retire. I want to have a word with you alone."

"What's the matter with you lot? Can't trust each other?"

A flash of annoyance crosses his gaze. I hit a nerve.

"I didn't want him to hear what I'm going to tell you."

"Why is that?"

"It has to do with your brother."

My blood runs cold. I sit up at once, stupidly showing my hand. He now knows I can move again. He doesn't step back though. Instead, he watches me with shrewd eyes.

"The wolfsbane has left your body already."

"Not completely."

"You were hoping to catch one of us off guard and attempt to escape."

I shrug. "That's the most logical train of thought."

"I'm glad you didn't try. It'd be foolish. You might escape this room, but you'd never see the outside world before you met the blade of one of my uncle's soldiers."

"Do you intend to keep me a prisoner here forever?"

He clasps his hands behind his back, appearing relaxed. "That depends."

"On what?" I arch my eyebrows.

"On where your loyalties lie. With your brother or your pack."

My heart squeezes in my chest. He does know about Karl's fate.

"I have no pack," I grit out. "Tell me where my brother is."

He doesn't answer immediately as he watches me like a hawk. This vampire is cunning. I need to be careful with him.

"He's not far from here," he finally replies. "I understand he was punished severely and cast out to die."

I blink fast, fighting the tears that have gathered in my eyes.

"He was taken by one of you. Why?" I ask.

His jaw becomes tense for a moment. *What does he know?* He moves away, pinching the bridge of his nose. His back is to me, and he left the door to this room unlocked. He knows I won't try to escape without getting all the information he has about Karl.

"It seems he assisted my sister during last week's battle," he replies as if it pains him to say the words. "She felt the need to repay the debt by warning him that my uncle intends to put a stop to the meeting between the wolves and the dragons."

"Son of a bitch. Karl, you idiot," I mutter under my breath.

The vampire looks over his shoulder. "You're not going to cast the blame on her?"

I raise an eyebrow. "Do you want me to?"

"Naturally not, but I can't say she doesn't have culpability in what happened to your brother."

"True, but no one forced Karl to help her in the first place." I push myself off the cot. "I need to go see my brother."

"I can't take you to where he is. It's daylight now."

"You can tell me, I don't need you to escort me."

He smiles wickedly. "Nice try. You're not going anywhere. As for your brother, we'll bring him here by nightfall."

"So you're just going to keep us both prisoners? Is that your endgame?"

"I can't tell you what my endgame is, but if I were you, I'd take the time you have now to think about what you want out of your new reality. I can't imagine life is easy for outcast wolves."

I narrow my eyes. "Do not pretend to care about my fate, bloodsucker. You want something from me and Karl."

"Perhaps. Now eat and rest. I'll be back after sunset."

He walks toward the door, unconcerned about his safety. I could take him now, but he wasn't lying when he said I wouldn't make it far. The best course of action is to heed his words. Eat, rest, and think of a plan to rescue Karl.

Sixteen

MANU

ITALY, 1520

I wake up from a pleasant dream, only to come to the realization that it wasn't a figment of my imagination. Karl's arm is wrapped around my waist, and his leg is covering mine. He shifts behind me, pulling me closer to his body. He's warm and hard in all the right places, and I melt against his frame. I still can't believe this is real. When his arousal presses against my butt, it brings a satisfied smile to my lips.

"Good morning, Princess," he whispers in my ear.

"It's not morning anymore."

He chuckles, then kisses my neck right below my ear, giving me goose bumps. "It will take a while to get used to this new routine."

I turn around in his arms so I can see his face. "Are you saying you're willing to switch to my nocturnal schedule?"

"You sound surprised. You're my mate. I'll be awake when you are."

As much as I would love to bask in the feel of his arms around me, I can't keep the worry from consuming me now. I'm his *mate*. The word drops between us like a crushing boulder.

"What's wrong?" he asks when he notices my frown.

"We need to talk about that."

He leans back, his gaze going from smoldering hot to cold in the blink of an eye. "I see."

"No, you don't see. This is all new to me, Karl. I haven't wrapped my mind around this whole mate business. What does that mean for us? I'm a vampire, you're a wolf shifter, and right now, I can't say our species like each other very much."

"It's going to be okay." He runs his fingers through my hair, gazing into my eyes with tenderness.

I begin to relax until a knock on my door interrupts our moment.

"Rats!"

Quickly, I toss my legs to the side of the bed, get up, and slip on a robe. Karl gets out of bed too, but not as fast as me. In fact, he seems more than comfortable taking his time.

"You should get dressed too."

"If you insist, but I don't think me getting dressed will make much difference to whoever is outside your door."

"You're way too undisturbed for someone who's smack in the middle of enemy territory."

"I didn't realize we were enemies." He smirks.

"Vampires and wolves aren't exactly friends, are they?"

I hurry to the common area, leaving Karl behind. Once I'm near the front door, I can sense Lucca standing outside. I let out a breath of relief. At least it's not Ronan or my mother. I honestly don't know how I'm going to explain to them and Uncle Raphael that Karl is my mate.

I open the door and let Lucca in. His expression is troubled, but then he takes a deep breath and curses.

"For fuck's sake, Manu."

I pull the lapels of my robe closer together. "What?"

"He's here, isn't he?" He steps toward my bedroom, but I jump in his way.

"Lucca, calm down. Let me explain."

He stops abruptly and looks at me as if I said something insane. "Considering the situation, I'm extremely calm."

Karl walks into the room then, mercifully, fully dressed. Lucca's stance relaxes, and I believe as far as first meetings go, this isn't too bad. But everything changes as quickly as lightning. Karl's gaze becomes feral, and then he attacks Lucca, pushing him against the door and holding him by his neck.

"What did you do to my sister?" he growls.

"Release me, you filthy beast," Lucca grits out.

His voice is dangerously low, which means Karl had better listen if he wishes to live.

"Karl, please, let my brother go," I plead.

"He has my sister's scent all over him."

I take a moment to inhale deeply, and indeed, I pick up the scent of a female wolf. "Luc? What's going on?"

"I'll explain if this savage calms the fuck down."

I pull Karl by the back of his tunic and drag him away from Lucca. It's obvious I only manage that because he lets me. The aggression hasn't left his body though. He's a moment away from snapping again.

"Go on, Lucca," I urge. "Tell us why you have Karl's sister's scent on you."

To be fair, the scent is faint, but perhaps Karl has a better sense of smell than I do.

"Last night, we caught his sister in the forest near the fortress wall. We apprehended her and brought her in for interrogation."

"You imprisoned my sister?" Karl's voice rises.

"She's not in the dungeons, and she's as comfortable as we could make her."

"That's not good enough."

"Listen here, wolf," Lucca snarls. "She was caught trespassing, and she was lucky it was me, Ronan, and Dean she encountered and not soldiers from the Red Guard."

"Ronan knows she's here?" I ask.

Lucca turns to me. "Yes. It was thanks to him that we were able to catch her."

"How?" Karl cuts in. "Cheryl is the fastest wolf in our pack."

Lucca's expression closes off, but his eyes are guilty as hell.

"Did you hurt her?" Karl takes a menacing step in his direction.

"Ronan's blade was laced with wolfsbane. He nicked her. It was only a scratch. She's fine."

A vein in Karl's forehead throbs, and his eyes are now glowing yellow. Shit, I think he's on the verge of shifting.

"Karl, please. Calm down. Trust my brother. He wouldn't hurt her," I assure him.

"I can't say the same thing about his friend."

I open my mouth to defend Ronan, but I can't vouch for him. He did attack Karl in the cabin.

I turn to my brother. "Luc, you need to bring her here."

His eyebrows shoot to the heavens. "Mother knows about her. If you're thinking about sneaking her and your lover out, forget it."

"They're not going anywhere." I take a deep breath. *Here goes nothing.* "Karl is my mate."

Lucca's eyes widen. He stares at me without blinking for a couple of beats and then shifts his attention to Karl. "What fresh hell is this?"

"It's true. You can confirm with Solomon if you don't believe us," Karl replies.

Lucca begins to pace. "How is that possible? You're not even the same species."

"I don't know. The mating bond is rare among wolves, and it only happens when there's a great need for it."

Lucca stops and turns to Karl. "Say that again?"

"Which part?"

"The part about it only happening where there's a great need. Is that true?"

"Yes. Why would I lie?"

His gaze becomes calculating as he narrows it. "This is interesting. Don't go anywhere." He veers for the door.

"Where are you going?" I ask.

"You asked me to bring his sister here. That's what I'm going to do."

RONAN

I respected Lucca's wishes and stayed away from the female wolf's cell throughout most of the day. But the compulsion to visit didn't diminish. On the contrary, it has only increased. I couldn't rest for more than a couple of hours, so to keep sane, I went to the armory for some training.

It was no surprise that I found the large room empty. Everyone in the fortress who isn't obsessing about a beautiful female is resting as they should. Tonight, we're heading to Indigo Mountain to stop the treaty between the vampires and wolves from taking place.

I go through the sword form exercises three times before my muscles say it's time to stop. Hunger simmers in my gut, reminding me that I haven't fed for far too long. I head out, covered in sweat, and make my way to the feeding room, where human snacks wait for their turn to nourish us. Some of them know who we are; others have been enchanted and lured here by familiars. Both are compensated well for their services and then compelled to forget they were ever here.

Giacomo, a non-blueblood vampire, bows his head when he sees me enter the room. Vampires who aren't first or second generation are usually weaker and tend to find other occupations outside the king's army. Giacomo is responsible for the food supply in the fortress.

"Good evening, Master Ronan. I haven't seen you here in a while. You must be starving."

"I could eat." I curl my lips into a sardonic smile.

"We just received a group of lovely ladies. They haven't serviced anyone yet. The early bird gets the worm, as the humans say."

"Bring them in." I head for one of the private feeding rooms and take a seat.

Feeding is a highly arousing activity, and more often than not, it leads to sex. I haven't fucked any human since the disaster with Manu, but perhaps I should give in to my urges considering I'm on the verge of making another mistake with that female wolf.

Giacomo returns a moment later with three beautiful human girls. They're all young, and at least one of them is a virgin. That's the first one I dismiss. I've had my share of maidens, and if I'm going to fuck anyone tonight, I want them to know what to expect.

The two women standing before me are like night and day. One has pitch-black hair and skin that looks like bronze. Her body is full in all the right places, and the way she's looking at me with desire in her eyes tells me she wasn't compelled to come here. She knows what I am and what I want from her. She would be the ideal treat for tonight, but my mind has other ideas.

I pick the other woman, the one with milk-colored skin and strawberry-blonde hair. She's not afraid of me, and her eyes aren't dazed, but she's not ready to go down on her knees and suck my cock after she's done feeding me. She's here because she needs the coin. That makes it easier for me.

I know why I chose her. Her coloring is similar to the female wolf, which means not fucking her tonight is a great exercise in self-restraint.

I motion for her to sit on my lap. Her breathing catches when I circle her waist with my arm.

"Don't be afraid. It only hurts a little."

"I'm not afraid," she replies in a testy bark.

Right. Her effort to appear strong would be beguiling to me if another feisty female wasn't already occupying my mind.

I push her long hair off her neck and, without preamble, sink my teeth into her soft skin. Her blood is sweet with a hint of spices. It serves to nourish me, but it doesn't trigger any stronger emotions. Her initial coldness turns into desire, and her breathing becomes uneven. I could fuck her now if I wanted to, but once I've drunk enough, I send her away.

Giacomo returns as I'm rising from the chair. The sign of my arousal is obvious, which prompts the vampire to quirk an eyebrow.

"Done so soon, Master Ronan?"

I fix my pants. "Yes. It turns out certain needs are not easily satiated."

Ignoring the male's hint of confusion, I stride out of the room and make a beeline for the tower. Alarm bells are telling me this is a mistake. I've just fed without sexual release. My body already craves her. Going to see her now and not being able to do anything will be torture.

Right at the foot of the stairs leading to the towers, I catch her scent, strong as ever, and also Lucca's. He's taken her somewhere, and by the freshness of their scents, it was recently. I follow the trail they left behind, and with each step, my apprehension grows. When it becomes clear where Lucca took her, I curse under my breath. There's more than one wolf inside Manu's room, and the second scent I detect is of the male who was with her in the cabin last week.

Damn everything to hell.

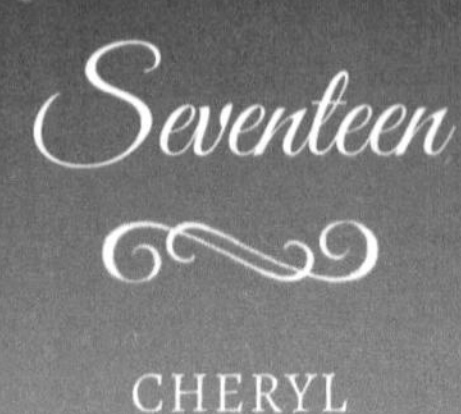

Seventeen

CHERYL

I'm wide awake when the dark-haired vampire comes to retrieve me. I can't say I was able to close my eyes for a second, even though it would have been wiser to rest. I don't know what the future holds for me. I might still have to fight to get myself out of this mess.

When I hear the door unlock, I stop my pacing and prepare to flee if the need arises. But as soon as Lucca enters the room, I smell Karl's scent all over him.

"You were with my brother."

"Yes. It turns out he's here too. I didn't know."

"Did your sister kidnap him? Where is he?"

He raises his hands, palms up. "Calm down. Your brother is fine." He smirks. "More than fine. I've come to take you to him."

I narrow my eyes. "He'd better not be in the dungeons."

Lucca laughs and then shakes his head. "He's definitely not in the dungeons."

I have no idea what to make of his reaction, but I follow him out of the room nonetheless.

"We'd better hurry before the fortress is fully awake," he says. "I don't want to have to explain your presence to any guard."

"I have a feeling you don't need to explain yourself to anyone."

"What makes you say that?"

"You feel different than your blond friend and that idiot with the arrow."

Lucca looks at me sideways. "How?"

"You smell different."

"You can tell the distinctive nuances among vampires just by our scent?"

"Of course. I'm a wolf. I don't know why you sound so surprised."

"To be honest, you're the first wolf shifter I've had a conversation with. I've seen you on the battlefield, but only in wolf form."

"You're the first bloodsucker who I've exchanged words with too. Well, you and your ogre friend."

"My ogre friend?" He chuckles.

I have a reply on the tip of my tongue but don't have a chance to say it. We've stopped in front of heavy double doors, and Karl's scent is coming strong from inside the room.

Lucca knocks first, but instead of waiting for a reply, he pushes the door open and strides in. I follow closely, my eyes searching for Karl frantically. I was expecting many things, but seeing him cozying up with a female vampire was not one of the scenarios I guessed.

"What the hell?" I say.

Karl steps away from the brunette with a look of shock on his face.

"Cheryl. You're okay." He cuts the distance between us and pulls me into a tight embrace. "I was so worried about you."

"Really? It didn't look like it." I ease back to glance up. "What happened, Karl?"

My question is loaded and could mean many things. But my

brother and I share a deep connection; I don't need to elaborate for him to understand exactly what I want to know.

"Dietrich happened. You were right about him. I should have paid more attention. He obviously had been poisoning Father against me for a long time. I wasn't given the chance to explain my side of things."

"And what was your side of things?" I look over his shoulder, my eyes landing on the female vampire, who looks a little like Lucca.

"Your brother helped me during the battle last week, and I came over last night to warn him about my uncle's plans to put a stop to the alliance between your pack and Larsson," she answers.

"Dietrich saw us together and was quick to twist the story to benefit him," Karl continues. "I was ambushed in the forest by his accomplices and taken prisoner. When I arrived in the village, Father had already made up his mind that I was a traitor and deserved to be punished as such."

I gasp. "Oh, Karl. I'm so sorry. Mother drugged me with wolfsbane. I would have put a stop to it if I could."

"No, you'd have been strapped to the pole and flayed alongside me. Mother saved you."

Tears prick my eyes. I shake my head, refusing to accept that my mother's actions came from her desire to protect me. She's awful, just like everyone else in that pack. If she cared about us, she wouldn't have let Father punish Karl.

"It doesn't matter. They tried to take you away from me. I'll never forgive them for that."

Karl's jaw hardens. He glances at the female vampire and then at her brother. "We have no loyalty to the pack. Whatever your uncle needs from us, we'll do our best to help in exchange for protection."

I want to say I'm surprised by Karl's declaration, but I can't. Alone, we're vulnerable and easy prey to other predators.

While his offer could have come from that reasoning alone, I notice something different about him. It's the way he seems aware of Lucca's sister at all times, even when he's looking at me.

I step away from his embrace. "What's going on here?"

"What do you mean?"

"You and that vampire."

"The name is Manu," she says.

I watch them closely. Karl can't hide the way he looks at her with adoration in his eyes.

"How long have you been lovers?" I ask.

He lets out a heavy sigh. "Cheryl, Manu is my mate."

The room begins to spin suddenly, making me dizzy. I press a hand to my chest, trying to ease the sudden ache there. Karl can't possibly be mated to a damn vampire. He can't. That's probably the worst fate that could have befallen him, worse than being betrayed by his pack. He doesn't deserve this.

The door bursts open, and in comes the blond vampire, oozing anger and bad intentions.

"The hell she is," he says.

I'm not done grilling my brother yet, but this asshole's attitude pisses me off. I whirl on the spot.

"Who the fuck do you think you are to tell anyone whether they're mates or not?"

My question seems to take him aback. His eyebrows arch, almost meeting his hairline. He opens and shuts his mouth like a fish out of water, but no sounds come forth.

"Great entrance, Ronan. How did you know we were having a meeting?" Lucca asks.

"I followed her scent." He points at me.

"Creepy much?" I cross my arms and glower.

His eyes narrow to slits, but in the end, he doesn't reply.

"It's not likely you can keep a secret from Ronan anyway, Luc. Might as well tell him the truth." Manu sighs. "Yes, Karl and I are mates."

"How does that even happen?" he asks. "You're not—"

"Of the same species," Manu and Karl say at the same time.

Hell, they're already picking up on each other's thoughts.

"It doesn't matter what they are. This is a situation we don't need right now," Ronan retorts.

"Actually, this couldn't have happened at a better time," Lucca chimes in. "Maybe we can prevent the alliance between their former pack and Larsson without shedding blood."

"You want to use my bond as a tactical advantage in war?" Manu asks.

"Don't sound so offended. I'm trying to help here. Just because you got yourself mated to a wolf shifter doesn't mean Uncle will be happy about it. I'm building the case for why he shouldn't execute the wolf siblings on the spot."

My blood runs cold. I hadn't stopped to consider that the hatred between vampires and wolves ran that deep. I thought our conflict was new, all thanks to the vampire wars.

"The king isn't going to kill them," Ronan replies.

"Of course he won't," I say. "I'd slash his throat open before he could lay his hands on us."

Ronan tilts his head to the side. "Aren't you cocky? May I remind you how easy it was to capture you?"

"You got lucky," I grit out

He tsks. "I think you're all bark and no bite."

My wolf awakens inside me. I take a step forward, allowing a partial shift. "I'll show you no bite."

Karl pulls me back, keeping me away from the ogre, but I'm still able to notice the effect my statement had on him.

I know desire when I see it, and the towering vampire is aroused by me.

Eighteen

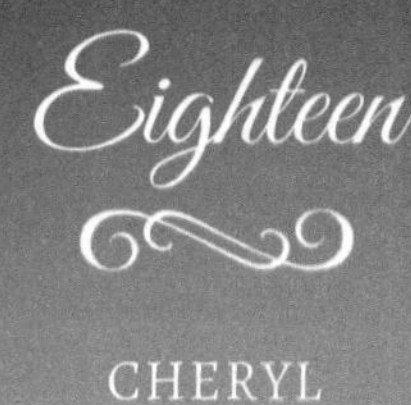

CHERYL

SALEM, PRESENT DAY

I run until I can't see the look of utter desperation on Ronan's face anymore. After all these centuries, she's the one he can't stop thinking about. It doesn't matter all the things she's done to hurt him, to hurt Karl. Manu Della Morte is still the female who owns his heart.

I had to get away from him. I'm resigned to my brother's fate. He was bound to the vampire princess before he decided to become her familiar. Ronan's devotion is by choice. As for me, I don't know why I can't eradicate him from my heart.

It's no surprise when I find myself in dragon territory. I shift back to human form before I leave the cover of the forest, glad the years of parading naked after a shift are gone. My clothes are crumpled from the battle in Ellnesari, but at least they're no longer covered in filth and blood, thanks to Nightingale magic.

I shouldn't be here. In the back of my mind, I know I'm toying with danger, but I need a distraction tonight, and Jagger van Praag is the cure for my bleeding heart. I run my hands over the front of my top, trying to smooth out the wrinkles, even if I know it's a futile attempt. I have no idea what my face looks like

"

though. The makeup I had on is most likely gone, and my hair must resemble a bird's nest.

I almost change course and retrace my steps, but fate has other ideas. Jagger is standing outside Ember Emporium, and he sees me before I can bolt. His smoldering eyes find mine, and it's impossible to stay immune to the heat in his gaze. My body reacts, remembering the many nights we spent together. Mind-blowing, earth-shattering orgasms—*that* will distract me from my pain.

Plastering a smile on my face, I stride toward him. He watches me suspiciously, and I don't blame him. The last time I saw him, I said it'd be the last. He was becoming too territorial, and that's not what I signed up for.

He crosses his arms over his chest, emphasizing the size of his biceps. Unlike his brother, who wears a suit and tie always, Jagger prefers a more casual look. Tonight, he's wearing a Black Veil Brides T-shirt that stretches across this chest and allows me to see all the intricate tattoos on his arms. It's impossible to look at him and not drool. The dragon is built like a rock, a delicious mountain any woman would want to climb—and I have so many times.

An arrogant smirk blossoms on his lips. "Look what the cat dragged in." He gives me an elevator look, and when his eyes meet mine again, one of his eyebrows is arched. "What happened to you, darling?"

"I've been to hell and back, and I'm in dire need of a drink."

His gaze narrows. "And you came all the way to Ember Emporium for it? What's the matter? The royal bloodsuckers don't have any alcohol handy?"

"I've had my fill of vampires."

"Like you had your fill of dragons last week."

Gone is the arrogant smirk. He's openly glowering.

I sigh. "Can we not do this right now? I came because I need a drink and a friend."

His eyebrows arch. "Oh, we're friends now? I thought I was nothing but a hookup, a boy toy for you to use when it suited your needs."

"Don't play the victim card, Jagger. It doesn't suit you. We both used each other. I never said I wanted more."

"Fair enough, but I don't want to be your booty call any longer. If you have an itch to scratch, you'd better find someone else to ride."

His attention shifts to a spot behind me, and his face twists into a scowl. "There you go. Your knight in shining armor has come for you. Sleep with him. We both know that's who you really want."

"What?" I turn and curse under my breath.

Ronan is striding toward us, and judging by his posture, I don't think he came to pay a social visit.

Son of a bitch.

"You followed me?" I put my hands on my hips.

"You bet your ass I did."

He turns to Jagger, and I'm now caught between two pissed-off alpha males.

"Save your murderous glare, bloodsucker. She's all yours." Jagger veers toward Ember Emporium and disappears inside.

"Come on, Cheryl. Let's go," Ronan demands.

"Excuse me? What makes you think I'm going anywhere with you?"

He steps into my space and brings his nose close to mine. "You're coming with me now. I'm done giving you the freedom to sort your shit out."

"You're not the boss of me."

I should step back. Being this close to him and not being able to do anything is torture. But apparently I'm a glutton for punishment, because I stay put.

He laughs without humor. "I *am* the boss of you. I'm your sire, and you *will* obey me!"

I feel the power in his words, and the compulsion to blindly bow to his will takes hold of me. The sting of betrayal pierces my chest, robbing me of air.

"You promised you'd never use your powers on me like that. You gave me your word," I say through the lump in my throat.

He finally leans back, but he's still much too close to me.

"Things have changed. I thought I could trust you to make good decisions, but now your reckless actions are a hindrance to everyone."

"*My* reckless actions? I've done nothing save clean up after the mess you guys made—more specifically your precious Manu. That's why you're here, isn't it? Karl sent you because he's too worried about his *master*," I say the last word with disgust.

"I'm here because I can't focus while I'm worried about you."

I scoff. "Please. If you ever truly cared about me, you wouldn't have—"

Shit. I've said too much. I can't bring myself to tell him that I know what he and Manu did. That their actions killed my brother's spirit and broke my heart to pieces.

"Why should I go back? It's not like I'm needed. You can figure out a way to return to Ellnesari without me."

A flash of hurt crosses his eyes, but it comes and goes too fast. He tears his gaze from my face to look at our surroundings.

"We've lingered here too long. We shouldn't be talking about private matters out in the street."

He makes a motion to grab my arm, but I step away from him.

"Don't touch me!"

The few dragon shifters who are hanging out in front of Ember Emporium are now watching us closely. Most are glaring in Ronan's direction. I don't have any illusions that they care about my safety, but for a while, I was constantly seen by Jagger's side. They might intervene if they think I'm in trouble just to save their asses with their boss.

Ronan rubs his face. His frustration sweeps over me, overwhelming my own emotions. He doesn't let me sense his feelings often, only when he's losing it.

I turn around and walk away from the dragon lair, angry at myself now for the tears that are turning my vision blurry.

Ronan follows closely, but he has better sense than to open his piehole.

I came here to run away from my past, but that's impossible when the reason I'm immortal is the asshole vampire who turned me.

Nineteen

KARL

ITALY, 1520

This is all happening so fast. I wish I'd had more time to discuss matters with Manu privately before we were forced into a meet-the-family situation. So far, only Lucca seems to be on our side. I know my sister too well to guess the nature of her thoughts. She isn't happy, and it will take time for her to get used to the changes in our lives. I'd feel the same way if the situation were reversed.

Ronan is another matter. I don't doubt he'd chop my head off if given the chance. His possessive reaction toward Manu was a declaration of war in my book. He obviously doesn't know how dangerous it is to get between mates.

Manu and I walk side by side toward the king's throne room. Lucca thought it was best to let his uncle know about the situation sooner rather than later. He's under the impression that I know all the details about the meeting between my father and the dragon king, but he couldn't be more mistaken. I was not privy to that information since, instead of attending the council meeting, I was arrested and accused of treason.

Lucca walks ahead with Cheryl by his side, and Ronan brings

up the rear. It feels like I'm being escorted to my execution, not a private meeting with the vampire royal family. Though it could very well be a trial that will end with my head on the chopping block.

Two bulky guards stand in front of the heavy double doors. They bow their heads in deference to Lucca and Manu but keep their curious gazes on Cheryl. She keeps her chin high and her shoulders squared. No surprise there. She'll never cower in front of anyone. I hope she knows better and keeps her mouth shut during the meeting with King Raphael.

The guards open the doors for our group and stand aside. I don't know what to expect, and my heart is reacting accordingly. Manu reaches for my hand and squeezes tightly. I turn to her, and immediately heat and yearning hit me. The urge to mate is intense, and it doesn't care that I'm about to meet her uncle and mother. Her warm brown eyes swim with desire. Hell, it's not only one sided, but why should it be? She's my mate, after all.

Heavens help me.

Cheryl looks over her shoulder, her face twisted into a scowl. "What are you doing? Tone it down."

"It's not like I have any control over it," I grit out.

In a move I couldn't foresee, Cheryl whirls around and punches me in my stomach. With a grunt, I drop Manu's hand to clutch my midsection.

"What the hell!" I wheeze.

Manu takes a step forward, ready to come to my defense, but Ronan holds her back.

"There. Now you're not thinking about fucking your mate in front of her family anymore," Cheryl replies.

Lucca clears his throat. "Shall we proceed?"

Still glaring at Cheryl's back, I follow them into the throne room. This time, I keep my hands to myself. As much as Cheryl annoys me, she did help clear my head from the mate-lust fog.

There's not much difference between this room and the rest of the fortress that I've seen so far. The dark stone walls make everything somber and sinister, paired with the glow from the torches. Large tapestries hang from them, depicting similar symbols and patterns. There aren't many windows, and the few present are narrow and nowhere near the throne. Heavy curtains drape them, and I wonder if that's enough to protect the vampires from the rays of sunlight.

The king is a massive male with dark hair and a short-cropped beard. His dark eyes are intense and remind me of Manu's. I try to get a read on him, but his expression reveals nothing. It's almost like he's made from stone.

A second throne is set next to his, and there sits Manu's spitting image save for the emerald-green eyes. They could be mistaken for twin sisters. She was young when she became a vampire, probably the same age as Manu is now. Unlike wolf shifters, vampires don't age, and the notion fills my head with dread. I'll grow old eventually, wither and die. Will Manu stay with me and watch old age cripple me? Do I want that fate for her?

"That's my mother," she tells me in a whisper.

"I figured as much." I keep my head facing straight ahead, but I can feel her inquisitive stare burning a hole in my face.

She can probably sense my turmoil now.

Lucca and Manu bow their heads once they stop in front of their uncle. I should copy them, but I'm caught up in my turbulent thoughts. Cheryl keeps her spine straight, and not even when the king tries to level her with his intimidating stare does she cower.

"What's the meaning of this, Lucca?" King Raphael asks finally. "Your mother told me you had apprehended one wolf shifter, and now you appear before me with two."

Manu takes a step forward and stops next to her brother. "It's better if I explain, Uncle, since it's my story to tell."

Her mother cocks her head to the side as she studies Manu. Then she looks at me. I don't know what she sees, but a sudden gasp escapes her lips.

"No," she breathes.

The king turns to her. "What's the matter, Natalia?"

The female shakes her head but keeps her lips sealed shut. Her eyes, though, they're troubled.

"She must sense my bond, Uncle," Manu says.

His eyebrows arch. "Bond? What bond?"

"Karl is my mate."

The king's expression doesn't change. He doesn't blink either. As for Natalia, her skin seems to grow pale.

"How is that possible?" the king finally asks.

"We don't know," I say.

"How did you meet?" Natalia clutches the arms of her throne in a vise grip, turning her knuckles white.

"We met during the confrontation with Tatiana's forces last week," Manu replies. "Karl helped me."

Manu and I take turns explaining the following events. When I recount what my father did to me, Cheryl's rage becomes a palpable thing. She doesn't utter a single word though, which is a blessing at least.

King Raphael and his sister remain silent for a while after we finish telling our story. The king still wears his indecipherable mask, but Natalia shows her emotions openly. Too bad there are too many for me to be able to tell where she stands.

"What now?" Manu breaks the silence.

The king rises from his throne and walks over to stand in front of her. "Are you happy with your new situation?"

"Yes," she replies without hesitation and then turns to me. "Very much so."

"What about you, Karl? Are you prepared to forget your ties of blood to join our family?"

"No," I say, surprising Manu. "I will never forget my blood ties for as long as Cheryl lives. But if you're referring to my father's pack, they're dead to me just like I'm dead to them."

The king nods and then looks at my sister. "What about you, child? You weren't branded a traitor or cast out."

"I cast myself out. My loyalty is to my brother. I'll follow him wherever he goes. If his destiny is by the vampire's side, then that's also my fate."

"Manu," Natalia cuts in. "Do you understand the ramifications of taking a wolf shifter as your consort?"

Manu raises her chin. "If you're referring to the scandal my relationship with Karl will bring, I'm prepared to deal with it."

Natalia shakes her head. "That's not what I meant. Are you prepared to watch your mate grow old and die?"

CHERYL

My heart breaks at the sadness that takes over my brother's face as the truth sinks in. I wasn't touched by the magic of the mating bond, but I can guess it's the strongest feeling a wolf can have for another.

My sentiment extends to Manu as well, even if she is who she is. Her fate is worse than my brother's. She's immortal, after all.

"There may be a way to circumvent that," Lucca pipes up.

"What do you mean?" Natalia asks.

"Luc, please don't," Manu says feebly, not meeting anyone's gaze.

Ignoring his sister, he takes a step forward. "If the wolf wishes, he could become Manu's familiar."

Natalia's eyes widen. "That's... that's absurd!"

"I agree," I say. "Karl, you can't possibly entertain that idea. You'll be bound to her forever."

He turns to me. "I'm already bound to Manu. She's my mate."

"But then you'll become her servant!"

"Enough!" King Raphael's voice booms in the throne room. "That's not a matter that needs to be discussed or decided right now. There are more pressing matters to attend to. What do you know about the meeting between your pack and Larsson van Praag?"

"I don't know much. I was cast out before I could learn of their plans," Karl says.

King Raphael turns to me. "What about you?'"

"Wolves believe females are only good for being dutiful wives and having children. I was not privy to any information either."

The king scoffs. "So both of you are useless to me."

I bristle. "I wouldn't be so quick to dismiss us just yet."

"If you have something of value to offer, speak now or leave my presence."

Hell, the vampire king is an even bigger asshole than the blond one.

"I know the dragon king demanded a gift from us."

"Cheryl, what are you talking about?" Karl asks me. "And how do you know that?"

I shrug. "I spied on Father. I learned a long time ago that if I want something badly enough, I need to go and get it myself."

Ronan makes a noise that sounds a lot like surprised appreciation. I glance at him, and sure enough, he's watching me with renewed interest. I shouldn't care about what he thinks of me. He's a perv and a bully, but pride spreads through my chest nonetheless.

"What type of gift did Larsson request?" Natalia asks.

"A maiden. He wanted one of our females, though I'm not sure to what end."

"Probably to use as a sacrifice," Lucca mutters.

Natalia glances at her brother, and it seems they share a secret message only with their eyes. Do they know what Larsson wants with a virgin female wolf?

"Who are they bringing?" Karl asks.

I snort. "Dietrich suggested me. He probably wanted to get both of us out of his way. I don't know now who they'll bring."

"That's good information, really good. Well done, Cheryl,"

the king says, surprising the hell out of me. "I know now what to do."

"Raphael, you're not considering—" Natalia starts.

"You were the one who begged me to find a way to stop the alliance between the wolves and the dragons without bloodshed. Now that the perfect opportunity has presented itself, you don't want me to use it?"

"We can't possibly offer the girl as bait."

"Whoa. What are you talking about now?" I ask.

"That's brilliant, Uncle," Lucca replies, ignoring my question.

Karl takes a step forward, body now coiled with tension. "You're not using my sister to entice a fucking dragon shifter."

"You want to arrive at the meeting point before the wolves do, don't you, my king?" Ronan says.

King Raphael nods. "Precisely. Karl will bring Cheryl, and we'll follow them but remain hidden. We need to leave at once if we hope to arrive before the real convoy does."

"No, that's madness," Karl retorts.

As I watch all the males in the room discuss a fate that very much depends on my cooperation, I think about the pros and cons. I've never seen a dragon shifter up close, however I trust that they're terrifying beasts and extremely dangerous. But I'm not one to cower in the face of danger. Besides, there's a major motivational factor in all this. I get to fuck up my father's plans, and in consequence, Dietrich's. I can already imagine the looks on their faces when they find out I made an alliance with the dragon king before they could.

"Wait. It's not such a crazy idea. It can work," I say.

Karl looks at me as if I've lost my mind. "You're willing to play the virginal sacrifice role?"

"Why not? As long as it's just for show. I don't actually intend to go through with it." I turn to the vampire king. "Just to be clear."

"We wouldn't leave you behind with those savage beasts. You have my word."

Lucca claps his hands together, smiling with glee. "Excellent. How many soldiers are we taking?"

King Raphael turns to him. "This is a covert operation. It will only be us."

"Not even Derek or James, my king?" Ronan asks.

"Derek is no longer on the premises, and I wouldn't risk exposing him anyway. As for James, he's unhappy about what happened to his son. I don't think rubbing Karl and Cheryl under his nose is the best course of action."

"I'm not coming," Natalia declares.

"Why not?" Manu asks.

Her face mirrors her brother's now. It's an impenetrable mask. "I have my reasons. Be careful out there. If Larsson discovers your duplicity, he'll make you pay dearly."

She walks out of the room, leaving us with that doomsday declaration. I have the feeling her advice is based on personal experience. But when did Natalia ever meet the dragon king?

Twenty

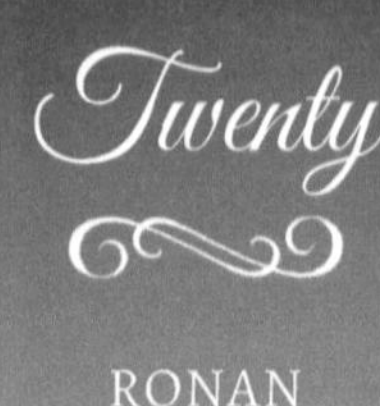

RONAN

ITALY, 1520

"I don't like this. I don't like this at all," I mutter under my breath.

Lucca steers his horse closer to mine. "Which part upsets you the most? The fact that we must depend on wolves for this deception to work or that my sister is now mated to one of them?"

I glare at him. "Both. Why are you acting so nonchalant about all this?"

"How do you want me to act? I've never had anything against wolf shifters. And now they're helping us. It's a win-win situation, in my opinion."

"I don't trust them." I look forward and glower at the back of Karl's head.

"Do you think Karl volunteered to be flogged on the slim chance Manu would find him and bring him to the fortress?"

"Of course not. But that doesn't mean he isn't going to betray us. What about his sister? She could be working for her father."

Lucca scoffs. "I think your animosity toward them is based on different things."

I bite my tongue because Lucca may be right.

We raced most of the way, but now that we're approaching Indigo Mountain, the terrain is steep, and we must advance with care.

King Raphael lifts his gloved hand, signaling for us to stop.

"What now?" I grumble.

"Fucking hell," a male mutters, and a moment later, Solomon steps from between two trees.

"You're difficult to track," the familiar says.

"What are you doing here?" the king asks.

"Saving your asses, that's what."

I turn to Lucca and give him a meaningful glance. "What did I tell you?"

"Don't jump to conclusions yet."

Solomon looks at Karl. "I see you've recovered well, young wolf."

Karl bows his head. "Thanks to you. I'll be forever grateful."

"Why have you come? Did something happen?" the king asks again, his tone more impatient.

Solomon nods. "Yes. I have news about the wolves. It seems there's a new alpha in town."

"What?" Karl blurts out too loud, upsetting his mount, which dances nervously under him.

Stupid wolf.

"Dietrich," Cheryl mutters. "He finally made his move."

"It seems so. I'm sorry," Solomon replies in a heartfelt tone.

If there's a new alpha, it means their father is dead. My outlook on the situation changes. I keep my eyes on Cheryl and watch her face go through a myriad of emotions. My chest feels tight, and once again, I want to offer her comfort. My reactions to the female are getting out of hand.

"My father got what he deserved," she says. "How does that affect our mission to fool the dragon king?"

"It seems a deal has already been struck between the wolves and the dragons," Solomon explains.

"When?" the king asks, but it's almost a growl.

"I don't know. We must make haste and reach Larsson as soon as possible."

"I don't understand," I say. "If a deal has been struck with the dragon king, what's the point of hurrying now?"

Solomon raises a brow. "I said there was a deal made, but I never said the new alpha made a deal with Larsson. It seems there's been a lot of cross dealings going on lately. The wolves made an arrangement with another dragon clan."

"How do you know all this?" Cheryl asks.

"I have my ways. Let's go. We don't have much time."

"Indigo Mountain is at least another hour away," Lucca says.

"Not if you run," Solomon replies.

King Raphael is the first to dismount from his horse. We all follow his example, and then, to my utter surprise, both Karl and Cheryl begin to undress.

"What are you doing?" I ask her. "You'll freeze to death."

"We're faster in our wolf forms."

She keeps her eyes locked on mine as she drops her clothes on the snowy ground. It's almost like she's daring me to look. I turn away instead of keeping her steady gaze. It's the coward's approach. I don't trust myself not to stare.

We tie our horses to trees, and then we rush up the mountain. Cheryl and her brother run alongside us, and I can't help but admire her wolf. Agile and lithe, she's a beauty I can't stop watching. But she's faster than all of us and soon takes the lead, vanishing from my view.

"She shouldn't run too far ahead," I tell Lucca.

"I think she can handle herself. Besides, she's keeping pace with Uncle."

Indeed, she's running next to the king. Solomon also decided to switch to his animal form, but his short legs can't keep up with us. Manu bends over and picks him up.

Oh, I bet he's loving that. We won't hear the end of it later.

I know we're getting near Indigo Mountain when the magic

that surrounds the place reaches us. Instead of slowing down, King Raphael increases his pace. I'm not sure if it's wise to rush ahead, but he's the king, and I have to trust his judgment.

The whoosh of giant wings is the only warning we get before fire rains down on us.

"Take cover!" the king orders.

I jump to the side, missing a jet of flames by a hair. The entire forest is set ablaze despite the trees being covered in snow. The roar of the dragon muffles the sound of our shouts and screams.

In the chaos, the first person I try to find is not Manu, Lucca, or the king. It's Cheryl. I don't know what that means, but there's no time to analyze my reaction. A fiery beast is intent on turning us into ashes, and surviving the inferno around us is all I should think about.

KARL

There was no warning that a massive dragon was near us. Cheryl and I should have been able to hear its wings way sooner than we did. I suspect magic is behind it. We scattered when the first attack came, but now it's time to regroup and find cover.

I look for Manu and spot her next to Lucca, not far from me. She turns in my direction and then drags her brother with her. One worry is lifted from my chest, but it's not enough to make me relieved.

"Cheryl! Are you okay?" I ask through our telepathic connection.

"I'm fine. And you?"

"Yeah. Where are you?"

"I don't know. There's fire everywhere."

The roar of another dragon raises my hackles.

"Fuck. Another one. Where are they coming from?" Lucca yells.

"They came out of nowhere." Manu looks at the sky.

I wish I could shift back so I could hold her in my arms and talk to her, but I'm needed in my wolf form.

Straight ahead, King Raphael appears and signals us to follow him.

"Do you see the king?" I ask Cheryl.

"No. Ugh!"

"Cheryl!"

The channel goes silent.

Manu and Lucca have already started making their way to the king, but I turn around and go after Cheryl. My bond is pulling me in the opposite direction, splitting my loyalties in half. I'm torn between finding my sister and protecting my mate.

The second dragon sweeps nearby, and I know if the winged beast aims its fire jet at me, there's no way I'll be able to escape. Heat comes from above, but I'm not the target. The second dragon is going after the first.

"Karl!" Manu calls my name, much too close.

I slow down and look back. She's running toward me instead of fleeing the scene. I'd yell at her, but I can't. I also can't move until she catches up with me.

"What is it, Karl?" she asks, frantic.

The howling of several wolves answers for me, and immediately rage courses through my veins. It's the call of traitors coming to finish the Eriksson line off.

Not tonight.

I surrender to my wolf's thirst for vengeance and take off toward the sound.

There's no sign of Cheryl anywhere, but my wolf now has a target. I spot Dietrich first, and without a second thought, I attack.

Twenty-One

MANU

ITALY, 1520

We were supposed to follow my uncle out of this inferno, but the moment I felt Karl wasn't following me, I had to turn around and go after him. I don't care about the danger. I'm not going anywhere without him. The mating bond magic is at work, but as he said, it doesn't matter. The feeling is real, probably the most real thing I've ever felt in my entire life.

At first, I was sure Karl was going after his sister, but then I hear the howling of several wolves. I unsheathe my blade and prepare to battle. If wolves are here, they aren't friendly.

It doesn't take long for me to locate Karl. He's engaged in a vicious fight with a wolf that's considerably larger than him.

My heart squeezes tightly in my chest as fear pierces through it. Karl is young and feral, but the other wolf has the size advantage. I can't help him though. That's his fight. From my periphery, I see a wolf break from the group and run toward me. I don't move until the beast pounces. Then I turn, swinging my sword with all my strength to catch it in the air. I cut it in half.

A snarl sounds behind me, and I barely have time to pivot and

"

block the attack. The wolf tries to sink its teeth into my armor and fails. I hit its head with the pommel of my sword, getting a satisfying crunch when its skull caves in.

The roar of two dragons fighting nearby makes the ground tremble. The forest around us is burning; soon the circle will close, and we'll be trapped. I hear Lucca shout and then find him slashing through a couple of wolves as he makes his way toward me. There's no sign of Ronan or Cheryl though. I hope they're okay.

A whimper of pain breaks through the noise. Instinctively, I know it was Karl who made that sound. He's on his side, bleeding from several cuts. The other wolf is hurt as well, but he's still standing and currently aiming to deliver the final blow.

"No!" I yell as I break into a run with my sword raised.

The wolf turns to me and peels his lips back, showing his sharp teeth. Then he starts in my direction, only to be stopped by Karl, who got back up. He clamps his jaw around the bigger wolf's neck and takes him down. The savagery of the attack makes my blood sing. That's my mate, avenging his undeserving father. He thrashes the piece of shit around, slashing his throat open. A pool of blood quickly forms around them, but Karl doesn't stop until his enemy's head detaches from the body.

"Manu!" Lucca yells a warning.

I turn around, sword at the ready, and slice the wolf who was already up in the air, ready to bite my neck. Breathing hard, I glance around me to make sure all the wolves have been dealt with. I only see carcasses on the snowy ground.

A sharp pain in my chest makes me return my attention to Karl. He's down again, bleeding even more. I rush to his side and drop to my knees.

"Karl... please don't die. I just found you."

He moves his head and nudges my leg with his nose.

"Is he okay?" Lucca asks, coming to stand next to us.

"I don't know. He has so many wounds. He needs a healer."

Lucca bends over and picks him up. "First, we need to get out of here."

The fire still rages, but the dragons are no longer fighting on top of us. As Lucca begins to move, Karl whines and squirms.

"We can't leave. Cheryl and Ronan are still here somewhere," I say.

"We're here," Ronan calls from behind us.

He has Cheryl with him, and she's changed back to human. His cloak is wrapped around her body. The most astonishing part of it all is that she's leaning against him.

"What happened?" I ask.

"A tree fell on me. The only way to break free was shifting back," she answers through a whimper.

Quickly, we move out of the circle of flames. When we locate Uncle and Solomon, they're staring, grim faced, at a slain dragon.

"Who was that?" Lucca asks.

"Draco De Jong," a stranger replies.

Through the smoke and fire, he approaches our group. He's as tall as my uncle and equally strong, with broad shoulders and arms that could break trees in half. I don't see any clothes, but his body is covered in dark soot, and it's almost as if he is wearing armor. There's no mistaking what he is—a dragon shifter.

"You're Larsson van Praag," Cheryl says.

"Yes. And you and your brother must be the Eriksson wolves. The last ones of your line."

Cheryl's eyes widen a fraction, the only reaction to the news. Until now, I thought only the alpha had been slain. It seems their mother was too. I lost my father years ago. I can relate to the pain, and it never gets easy.

"Karl is hurt badly. He needs a healer," I say.

Larsson turns his attention to Karl in Lucca's arms. "Yes. He's dying. I can feel his essence ebbing away."

His words cut like the sharpest blade.

"Where's Solomon?" Cheryl asks, searching around. "He helped Karl before."

"He was here a moment ago," Uncle replies.

"You shouldn't have come here, Raphael," Larsson says as if we didn't have more urgent matters on our hands.

"You shouldn't have tried to make a treaty with the wolves, Larsson."

"Shut up! Both of you," Cheryl orders, stepping away from Ronan's side. "I'm not going to watch my brother die while you two have a royal pissing contest."

Larsson's eyes glow bright yellow, but before he can make his next move, Solomon comes running toward us, and he's not alone. A man wearing black leather and a black hooded cloak is with him. Immediately, I know he's not an ordinary human. He reeks of magic, but not just any kind. Dark magic.

"What is he doing here?" Larsson asks.

"Nice to see you too, dragon," the man says.

"He's here because I asked him to come," Solomon cuts in. "Now, let him help the wolf."

"Fucking hell. He's a rogue mage," Lucca mutters as the man comes closer.

Cheryl jumps between him and her brother. "Stay away from him with your evil sorcery."

He sighs. "I don't have time for this, little wolf. My time is valuable. Get out of my way, or your brother surely will die."

I grab Cheryl's arm. "Let him help Karl."

Her eyes are round with fear. "Even if it means using dark magic to do so?"

"Yes."

Cheryl glances at the impatient face of the mage and then at Karl. Finally, she steps away.

The mage gives Karl's wound a cursory glance and then turns to me. "Take him from your brother."

I find his request strange, but I don't argue. Once I have Karl in my arms, the mage rests his hands on my shoulders, and then the whole world is surrounded by a bright green light.

I hear Cheryl's scream, but it's muffled as if I'm hearing it from underwater. The light vanishes a moment later, and we're no longer in the forest near the Indigo Mountain but in a beautiful garden where the bite of winter doesn't touch us. As a matter of fact, I don't see snow anywhere.

"Where did you bring us?" I ask.

The mage doesn't answer; instead, he steps back and turns toward the gazebo straight ahead. There's someone there, a robed figure with long white hair. I can't tell if it's a male or female as they take the steps down and walk over to us. Their features are stunning and delicate, but despite the feminine angles, I sense him as a male. A Nightingale male.

"What have you brought here, Damiano?" the male asks.

"This wolf wishes to become the vampire's familiar."

"Wait. Karl didn't agree to that," I say.

The Nightingale furrows his eyebrows. "He's severely wounded."

"As usual, your penchant for pointing out the obvious is remarkable," the mage replies.

The Nightingale doesn't seem offended by the man's sarcastic comment. He stops in front of us and places a hand on Karl's forehead, closing his eyes.

"Hmmm. The wolf does wish to become your familiar, child."

"How do you know?"

"I can read his thoughts." He opens his eyes and stares at me with his unusual light-gray irises. "But I can't read yours. Do you wish to take him as your familiar?"

I haven't had time to process all that's happened to me in such a short period of time, but my mother's words come back to me. Karl is mortal, so he only has a few more decades to live before he departs this world. I'll have to bear an extremely long existence without him. I don't think I'll be strong enough to bear it.

"I... yes, I do."

"It's not an easy commitment, child. Think carefully. Once

the bond between an animal and a vampire is made, it can't be unbroken."

"He's not an animal," I grit out. "He's a wolf shifter."

"Yes, but the familiar bond will be made with his wolf side, not human."

"What does that mean?"

The Nightingale seems confused. "Exactly what I said."

"It won't make a difference in the outcome since Karl and his wolf are one and the same," the mage replies.

"What about our mating bond? Will it be affected?" I ask.

The Nightingale shakes his head. "I don't know. Your situation is unique. If you want to go ahead with it, I suggest we do it now. Your mate is hanging on by a thread. If he dies, there's nothing I can do."

I look at Karl and cup the side of his head. His eyes open, and even in his wolf form, I feel his love for me. He loves me, and I let that realization wash over me. I search in the depths of my heart for the truth, trying to ignore the magic of the mating bond, and discover that I've loved him since the first time I saw him in the forest, only I didn't know what it was.

"Yes, I want to go ahead."

Twenty-Two

KARL

My head is spinning as I watch Lucca pace back and forth in his living room. I can't believe we let the only two people who could find a way back into Ellnesari slip away. Who gives a fuck what the High Witch thinks? Surely we need Solomon's knowledge more than Isadora Leal does. Or maybe the first familiar is sick of our problems and used the High Witch as an excuse to leave. There was a time when he cared less about authority. I guess old age has taken the edge out of him.

Vivi is sitting next to Aurora on the couch opposite mine while Saxon and Vaughn have chosen to remain standing, but they're all sporting similar, concerned masks.

It's been an hour since we returned from Ellnesari. I don't know how long it's been for Manu in the other realm. Time doesn't move the same way here as it does there. If it did, all the vampires would have turned to ashes the moment we crossed the portal Rikkon created.

We haven't heard from Cheryl or Ronan yet, and that adds another set of worries to my long list. I hope Cheryl doesn't carve up more problems for herself and the rest of us. I'm all too aware of her involvement with Larsson's brother Jagger. To think that a few centuries ago, we trusted dragons as far as we could throw them. And now here we are, coexisting with them peacefully.

"I can't believe your brother didn't stay to help," Lucca mutters. "If he could bring us here, then I don't see why he can't open another portal into Ellnesari."

"My father gave him the ability for one trip only. You know that." Vivi rubs her temple as though she's trying to get rid of a headache.

"That's such BS. No offense, but the Nightingales are all a bunch of assholes even when they assist," Saxon retorts.

"Sadly, I agree with you," she says.

"How about you, Vivi?" I butt in. "You have your powers back. Can't you figure something out?"

She shakes her head. "No. My powers, like Rikkon's, are limited. Even to shut off Ellnesari completely from the human realm took the combined effort of several royal houses."

Aurora stands up suddenly. "There's only one thing left to do, then. I must get the answer from my new coworkers."

Saxon narrows his eyes. "Hell to the fucking no. I'm not ready to let you leave me and train with those warlocks yet."

She puts her hands on her hips. "Hell to the fucking no?"

Looking sheepish now, he rubs the back of his neck. "Eh, pretty please, don't leave me yet?"

I can see she's trying to stay mad at him, but she's losing the battle.

She finally shakes her head. "I'm sorry, Sax, but I don't see any other option to find a way into Ellnesari now that the Taluah Mirror is gone."

"Let's not waste any more time, then," I say. "Where do we find your warlock friends?"

Aurora pulls from under her shirt an amulet that depicts two snakes, symbolizing infinity.

"What is that?" Lucca squints.

"This is what Ryker gave me to use when I was ready to join the brethren," Aurora replies.

"How does it work?" Vivi asks.

"I'm not sure. I haven't used it yet."

"No, but you can't take it off either," Saxon mutters under his breath.

Is he jealous of a piece of jewelry?

She gives him the stink eye. "Sax, you're acting like a child. I have to wear the necklace. What if I need to contact them out of the blue?"

He crosses his arms over his chest. "And I maintain my opinion that those assholes are using that amulet to spy on you."

"Can you shove your immaturity aside for one second and let your mate call for help?" I cut in. "In case you've forgotten, Manu is trapped in a fucked-up realm."

"Bite me, wolf boy. For a familiar who forgot your duties for centuries, your sudden concern is mega sus."

"Shut up, Saxon," Lucca interjects. "You *are* delaying things. Go on, Aurora, call them."

The annoying blondie finally shuts his piehole and lets his mate work. She scrunches her brows and stares at the object in her hand until it begins to glow from within, a bright green light that shines over her face. A moment later, her eyes glow the same color as the amulet. The whole green effect makes her look like the witch from *The Wizard of Oz*.

Magic leaks from the object and spreads at a rapid pace around the room. My skin tingles when the current touches my skin, and my wolf becomes restless.

A gust of strong wind sweeps the room, making Aurora's and Vivi's hair dance wildly around their heads. The magic reaches a crescendo, and then the whole room is enveloped in the green light coming from the amulet. I cover my eyes with my arm when the brightness becomes too much. The summoning magic recedes, but another kind takes its place.

Upon opening my eyes, I see a tall figure standing in front of the fireplace. He wears black from head to toe and the arrogant smirk I've come to associate with his kind.

"Aurora, I've been waiting for your call."

She nods once. "Hello, Ryker."

He looks around the room, raising an eyebrow. "I take it you've gathered all your friends to bid you goodbye?"

"Rora is not going anywhere with you," Saxon growls.

The warlock frowns. "I specifically told you only to use that amulet when you were ready to start your training."

"Well, I'm not quite ready to leave yet. There's been an emergency, and I need your help."

He lets out an exasperated sigh. "You didn't even begin your apprenticeship, and you're already abusing the power I gave you."

"Yeah, yeah." She waves her hand dismissively. "And who defeated Ashmedai when you couldn't? This untrained warlock here and her mate."

"Burn!" Saxon shouts.

God, was he always this immature?

Ryker pinches the bridge of his nose. "That's what I get for dealing with children. What is the emergency?"

"My sister is stuck in Ellnesari, and we need to get her back," Lucca replies.

"So it *is* true. You managed to cross into Ellnesari. We sensed a disturbance in the magic around Salem that felt a lot like a portal had been opened, but we didn't think anyone had actually managed that. Let me guess. You used the Taluah Mirror to do it."

"Yes, but the second time around, it blew into smithereens," Aurora says.

"The second time around?" His eyebrows arch. "You mean to say you've done it twice?"

"Yes. The first time, a member of Queen Maewe's court had the spell to open a portal using the mirror," Vivi replies.

"What happened the second time?" the warlock asks.

Aurora drops her gaze to her lap, blushing furiously now.

Saxon's lips curl into a mischievous smile. I fight the urge to roll my eyes.

"Saxon and Aurora got carried away during their portion of the spell," I reply. "Can you help or not?"

The warlock stares at me with his gaze narrowed for a couple of beats. "I cannot."

My stomach bottoms out, and my head begins to spin. If he can't help, and the two Nightingale heirs in our group can't either, then Manu will be stuck in Ellnesari forever. The very idea of never seeing her again rips my heart out of my chest. And I thought all these centuries apart from her were torture. At least I could see her whenever the pain became too much.

"So much for all your powers," Saxon grumbles, earning Ryker's glare.

"My magic only goes so far. To open a portal into Ellnesari, I need an amplifier, an object of power made by the Nightingales."

My spine goes rigid in an instant. I know who had such a relic. I can't believe it didn't occur to me until now. Maybe it was the gag spell Solomon put on me all those centuries ago.

I open my mouth to speak of it but find my tongue tied. *Damn it. It's still in place.* However, he did mention that someone with access to powerful magic could undo the spell. But how do I tell Ryker that when I can't speak of it?

"I need a piece of paper," I say.

Saxon raises his eyebrows. "What for?"

"I... I'm unable to say it out loud. I have to try another way."

Ryker stares at me through slitted eyes. "What's with you? I sense a block has been placed on your mind."

I open and shut my mouth, but the words won't come out.

Aurora jumps to her feet. "Holy crap. I can feel that too."

"What are you saying? Did someone put a silence spell on Karl?" Lucca asks.

I try to nod in confirmation, but I can't even do that. *Damn it. Solomon covered all his bases.*

Without asking, Ryker flattens his palm on my forehead.

Sharp pain spreads across my entire head, but I can't move away from the warlock.

"What are you doing to him?" Vivi asks.

"Lifting the spell put on him."

I curl my hands into fists and ride out the skull-splitting pain. It feels like the warlock's hand is now deep into my brain, yanking my neurons. I taste blood in my mouth and realize I bit my tongue. When he finally pulls back, I collapse onto my knees.

My eyes are shut, but I recognize Vivi's touch on my back. "Are you okay?"

My tongue is dry and glued in place. I can't answer her. I can barely hold on to my consciousness.

"Give him a minute, lass," Ryker says.

Before I can recover the ability to speak, sudden nausea erupts from the pit of my stomach. I push Vivi away and then turn on my side to puke my guts out.

"For fuck's sake. That rug is going to reek for weeks," Saxon complains.

My eyes and nose burn as I retch until there's nothing else in my stomach. Mortification sweeps over me when I glance around the room.

"I'm sorry about the rug," I tell Lucca.

He waves his hand dismissively. "Forget about the rug. Is the spell lifted?"

"Solomon has a miniature version of the Taluah Mirror," I blurt out.

No one speaks for several beats, and then Saxon breaks the silence. "I guess that answers your question, Luc."

"That sneaky weasel. No wonder he was in a hurry to leave after we returned from Ellnesari," Lucca says.

As much as I hate what Solomon did to me, I can't forget that he saved my life twice.

"Maybe he doesn't have it anymore. He let me use it before I became Manu's familiar."

Saxon rubs his chin. "Hmm, I'd bet a limb that he still has the mirror."

"So, what do we do now?" Vaughn asks, reminding me of his presence.

Ryker's eyes spark with determination and a little annoyance. "We have a little chat with your friend."

Twenty-Three

KARL

SALEM, PRESENT DAY

"All right, gather around," Ryker orders.

"What for?" Vaughn watches him suspiciously, crossing his arms over his chest.

He hasn't experienced the joys of traveling through warlock magic yet. He's in for a treat.

"You're going to transport us where Solomon is, aren't you?" I ask.

Ryker nods. "Precisely."

Saxon steps close to Vaughn and asks, "Do you enjoy roller coasters?"

"Yeah. They're fun. Why?"

He clasps him on the shoulder and smiles wickedly. "Then you have nothing to fear."

"I'm not afraid of anything," he retorts.

"You haven't lived long enough," Lucca pipes up. "Enough with the chitchat. If Solomon still has the Nightingale relic in his possession, we need to retrieve it now."

No one argues with his authoritarian tone. We form a circle

around Ryker, and then the warlock's magic surrounds us. His eyes glow an eerie green, making him look otherworldly. My last thought before my body seems to disintegrate in a million pieces is of Cheryl. Did Ronan find her? And was it wise to send the vampire after her? Their relationship is as turbulent as mine with Manu is, perhaps even more.

I expect Ryker to take us to Bloodstone Institute, but instead we drop in the middle of a forest. In the darkness, it's hard to tell which one.

"Holy hell," Vaughn exclaims, resting his hands on his knees. "That was nothing like a roller-coaster ride."

"I know." Saxon chuckles.

"Where are we?" Vivi walks away from the group to investigate our surroundings.

I take a deep breath but don't pick up any scent that would tell me our exact location. Ryker is already on the move though, and he doesn't bother to answer her. I follow the jerkface, not putting it past him to disappear from our sight on purpose.

"Man, he's not very friendly, is he?" Vaughn mutters behind me.

"I haven't met a warlock who is," I reply.

"That's not true. I'm not an asshole," Aurora butts in.

"No, but you haven't had your training yet," Lucca adds somberly. "I think it changes them, almost like it takes away part of their soul."

"What the hell, Luc?" Saxon complains. "Why would you say something like that?"

Aurora raises her chin stubbornly. "They've already taken much from me. I'm not going to let them change me on top of it."

I don't understand her comment, but when it comes to the magical community, the more powerful they are, the greater the sacrifices.

"Of course you aren't," Vivi says while glaring at Lucca.

He doesn't seem to notice or care about her death stare. He's preoccupied, more than ever. Of course, he does have a lot on his plate. His uncle's disease, the vampire community on the verge of another civil war, and now Manu acting like the selfish brat she is. Hell, I still can't believe she chose to remain in Ellnesari. What's her endgame? Revenge? I know they've all suffered at the hands of Queen Maewe, but to act so foolishly is a new low for her. Surely she must have known we wouldn't abandon her there.

"I thought we were going after Solomon," Saxon pipes up.

"We are," Ryker replies. "Apparently he has a second home."

"Why am I not surprised?" Aurora shakes her head.

We follow the warlock through thick branches until we reach a clearing with an old cabin in the middle.

"I didn't know this was here," Lucca says.

"It looks exactly like his dwelling in the old country," I add.

Light is coming from inside the building, which means someone is there. Ryker takes the lead and knocks on the door.

"I didn't know you had proper manners," Saxon says. "I thought your MO was to drop into people's living rooms unannounced."

"The old familiar has wards all over this property."

"Of course he does," I say.

Solomon opens the door slowly and only partially. "What do you want?"

"It seems you've been keeping a secret from everyone, Corvicus."

Ryker braces his hand against the door and pushes it open all the way. He strides in, and we quickly follow suit.

"To what do I owe the pleasure of this impromptu visit?" Solomon asks, eyeing all of us suspiciously.

I step closer. "The gag spell you put on me is gone. They know you have another Nightingale-made mirror."

His bushy eyebrows rise, meeting his hairline, but the surprise comes and goes in the blink of an eye. He releases a sigh, shaking his head.

"I knew you would figure out a way to remove it. But it's too late now. I no longer possess the mirror."

He veers toward a wooden table and pours himself a drink that smells awful.

"You'd better not be lying, Solomon," Lucca snarls. "My sister's life is at stake."

Solomon tosses the drink back and then looks over his shoulder. "Yes, and so is Karl's life. That's something you vampires always seem to forget."

"I didn't forget it," Lucca retorts.

"The familiar is not lying," Ryker chimes in. "He... *lost* it."

Solomon takes a step back, glaring at the warlock. "Stay out of my head, fiend."

"How could you have lost something so powerful?" Vivi asks.

Looking ashamed, he turns away and pours himself more of his stinky drink. "I lost a bet and had to give up the mirror."

"Son of a bitch." I pass a hand over my face.

Can we catch a fucking break?

"I would have come forth with the mirror if I still had it. Surely you know that," he continues.

"Who did you lose the mirror to?" Saxon asks. "Maybe we can get it back, or at least borrow it."

He snorts. "Good luck with that."

"Solomon," Lucca says with a hint of warning in his tone.

"Fine. I lost the mirror to the Elder dragon."

Looking around the room, it seems only Ryker, Lucca, and Vivi know who Solomon is referring to, and their matching grim expressions don't give me comfort.

"Who is the Elder dragon?" Aurora asks.

"She's the dragon who lives deep in the Indigo Mountain," Lucca says. "I've never seen her, but Uncle Raphael mentioned her name on a few occasions."

"She's an oracle for the dragons. Old and powerful and, most importantly, as mercurial as they come," Ryker replies. "Getting the mirror from her will require a miracle."

I press a closed fist against my forehead. "If the only way to open a portal to Ellnesari is using the mirror, we don't have any other choice. We must head to Indigo Mountain and deal with her."

"I can take you there, but I'd suggest leaving your girlfriends behind," Ryker says.

Aurora places her hands on her hips. "What kind of sexist bullshit is that?"

"The Elder dragon doesn't like females, but she has a weakness for pretty boys," Solomon answers. "Your chances of getting the mirror increase a tiny bit if you and Vivi aren't there."

"When you say the Elder dragon likes pretty boys, you mean she likes to hang out with them, right? Not eat them?" Vaughn chimes in.

Ryker cocks his head. "That depends."

"On what?" Saxon asks.

"On whether you piss her off or not."

Aurora crosses her arms. "I don't like this. I say we should all go. We can wait by the foot of the mountain."

"I don't advise it," Ryker replies. "The Elder dragon is not the only dangerous thing living in the area. It helps no one if your boyfriends have their attentions split."

"It'll be okay, Rora." Saxon steps in front of her and cups her cheek. "We'll be back before you know it."

"Vivi and Aurora will stay," Lucca says, his tone hard, which means that's his final word.

He's beginning to sound more and more like his uncle.

"I didn't agree to that," Vivi complains. "I'm no longer a damsel in distress who needs saving. I can handle myself."

It's becoming obvious that heading to Indigo Mountain without the girls will be impossible.

"I'll go alone," I say.

"What? Karl, you can't go by yourself. It's dangerous," Vivi retorts.

"Manu is *my* problem. If anyone has to risk anything, that person is me."

"You're forgetting that she's my sister," Lucca cuts in.

"I'm not. But you're needed here. If something goes wrong and you get hurt...."

My words drop in the room like a bomb. If Lucca dies, it's game over. Jacques will take over, and it'll be chaos. For better or worse, King Raphael's reign is what's kept the supernatural species living in peace. But whispers of conflict in Boston and other major cities in the country have been reaching Salem for a while now. The king has been absent for far too long, and the supernatural underbelly is getting restless. How long before they decide it's safe to wreak havoc and oust our existence to the entire world?

"Take me with you, Karl, for backup," Vaughn says. "I have nothing to lose, and no one needs me here."

"Vaughn, that's not true," Vivi pipes up.

He shrugs. "I know I'm a complication you didn't ask for. Who has time to train a newbie bloodsucker when the world is about to blow up in your faces?"

Ryker studies Vaughn for a moment. "It's not a bad idea to bring the young vampire. He's attractive enough. He can distract the Elder dragon with his pretty looks."

I don't want to think too much about what that entails.

"Fine, Vaughn can come," I say.

Ryker nods once. "Let's go, then. I've lingered here long enough, and I don't remember signing up to be at the vampires' beck and call."

"You can't open a portal inside my home, so shoo." Solomon makes the motion with his hands.

Ryker quirks an eyebrow. "Shoo?" He then grabs the male from the back of his collar. "You're coming with us."

Solomon struggles against Ryker's hold. "The hell I am. Let go of me, you brute."

The warlock ignores Solomon's protests and drags him

outside. With just a look, he commands Vaughn and me to move closer.

"What about us? How are we getting back to the house?" Saxon asks.

"You forgot how to walk?" Ryker cocks an eyebrow.

"We don't know where we are." Saxon throws his hands up in the air. "We could be miles from home."

"Stop being so dramatic," Solomon barks. "You're behind the institute. Head east and you'll find the main road."

I look around and can't say I recognize any of the trees or the scents in this forest.

"You've enchanted this area," I say as the realization sinks in. "That's why we can't pinpoint our exact location."

"Finally, someone figured it out." Solomon breaks free from Ryker's grasp and fixes his clothes. "I don't think the Elder dragon will appreciate me dropping by unannounced."

The warlock rolls his eyes. "She's going to appreciate it even less if I show up with a wolf shifter and a newly minted vampire. They need an introduction."

"Why can't you do it?"

Ryker's lips twist upward. "She likes me even less."

Twenty-Four

RONAN

Cheryl and I walked back home; she refused to run in her human form, and I didn't let her shift. She kept quiet during the trip, but she didn't try to hide the hatred she feels toward me. Our relationship has never been easy, even when I felt it was developing into something more. Then she changed. She began to hate me, and I never knew why. Despite being linked to her, she kept that part of herself shut off from me. It happened around the time Manu was cursed by Queen Maewe and rejected Karl.

Her silence during the trip back pains me, but I have a mission, which is to escort her back safely to the manor. It's bad enough we have to worry about Manu's safety. Cheryl, just like Manu, lets her emotions control her decisions. I must be a glutton for punishment for getting involved with both females.

Cheryl enters the house first and calls for her brother. We're met by Lucca and Vivi instead.

"Oh, thank heavens you guys are back," Vivi says.

"Where's Karl?" Cheryl asks.

"He left for Indigo Mountain," Lucca replies, not looking too happy about it.

Shit, that can't be good.

"What for?" I ask.

"It's a long story," Lucca replies, "but it seems the Elder dragon has another Nightingale-made mirror."

"And Karl went after it?" Cheryl's voice rises. "Is he insane?"

I turn to her. "Why do you say that?"

She tries to level me with a glower. I react with one of my own. *Two can play the hating game, sweetheart.*

"The Elder dragon is a petty, nasty creature," she replies. "Even the other dragons know to stay away from her."

I cross my arms over my chest, trying hard to tamp down my displeasure. "And how do you know so much about the Elder dragon?"

She narrows her eyes to slits. "Do you really want to know that?"

Fuck. As I suspected, she learned that from her dragon lover. Jealousy rears its ugly head again. I try to push it back to a place where I can't feel the sting of its savage bite.

"Solomon and Vaughn went with Karl," Vivi says.

Cheryl snorts. "Oh, that's fantastic. Vaughn is a baby vampire, and Solomon is... Solomon. He can't fight the Elder dragon alone."

Vivi's expression twists into one of guilt. She turns to Lucca. "Maybe we shouldn't have let them go alone."

"You think?" Cheryl snaps. "I need to go after them."

"What's done is done," Lucca replies. "We have to trust Karl will be able to handle the situation."

Wild rage erupts from Cheryl's core. It's so potent that it washes over me. She takes a step toward Lucca, ready to blow. Quickly, I grab her arm and pull her back.

"Settle down," I tell her.

I don't use my powers on her this time. I did promise I wouldn't ever try to control her in that manner, and it made me feel like an asshole for doing so earlier. In truth, I lost my temper. Seeing her with Jagger didn't sit well with me.

She yanks her arm free. "Quit telling me what to do."

"You can't go after them," Lucca says. "Ryker opened a portal, but he's unlikely to return here for a very long time."

"I can take Cheryl," Vivi announces.

"What? You're not going to Indigo Mountain," Lucca retorts. "Did you already forget the reason why you had to stay behind?"

She puts her hands on her hips and glares. "Are you really going to pull the controlling male card with me?"

"Yes, if it means keeping you from facing a psychotic three-headed dragon."

"I've faced way more dangerous beasts in my lifetime, Luc."

He steps into her personal space and cups her cheek. "I can't lose you, Vivi. I won't survive all of what's to come if you're not by my side."

"You're not going to lose me."

"God, can you stop with the lovey-dovey stuff? It's making me sick," Cheryl complains. "Now, how can you take me to Indigo Mountain, Vivi?"

"I can't open a portal like Ryker can, but I can walk the wind and take you with me."

"How many people can travel with you like that?" I ask.

Cheryl turns to me. "Why do you care? You aren't coming."

"You task me, Cheryl," I grit out.

"As many as I can connect with," Vivi replies. "I just need a clear picture of where I'm going."

"Have you ever been to Indigo Mountain, my love?" Lucca asks softly.

Her face turns pink. "Once. I was there when you were attacked by that dragon Draco or something."

Lucca's eyes widen. "You were there? Why?"

"What do you think?" Cheryl snorts. "Vivi was quite the stalker back then."

"I was not!" Vivi snaps. But considering how red her face is now, I'd say Cheryl is right.

"It's okay, love. I don't mind," Lucca replies with a cheeky smile on his face.

"You could have at least helped us." Cheryl crosses her arms.

Vivi's eyebrows shoot up. "I did. I told Larsson what was happening."

Lucca turns to her. "I didn't know you had a relationship with the dragon kingpin back then."

"I didn't either until recently. And I wouldn't say I had a relationship with him. I just knew he didn't have bad intentions toward your group and the other dragon did."

"I'd love to stay here and reminisce, but we don't have much time," Cheryl chimes in. "Let's go before the Elder dragon fries my brother."

Vivi nods. "Right. Give me your hand."

Lucca touches her shoulder. "Vivi, you're not going to Indigo Mountain alone. If you take Cheryl, you'll have to take me as well."

"And me," I say.

Cheryl seethes. "You're really determined to be a pain in my ass for all eternity, aren't you?"

I grin. "You begged me for it."

Her nostrils flare, and once again, I'm hit by her anger. What I said was cruel. She did beg, but I would have done it even if she didn't. It was either that or lose her forever.

"Let's go before Aurora and Saxon show up and decide they need to come as well," Cheryl says.

"Where are they now?" I ask.

Lucca quirks an eyebrow. "Where do you think?"

I shake my head. No doubt I'm distracted if I couldn't figure that out on my own. They spend more time in the bedroom than anywhere else.

"We aren't going anywhere unprepared," Lucca says.

"How do you plan to prepare to meet a dragon?" Vivi asks.

"A couple swords will do," I answer. "We don't want to appear hostile, so anything more than that would be overkill."

"A quick trip to the weapons room, then," Lucca says.

What was supposed to be a fast in-and-out situation in the weapons room turned into a half-hour discussion about which sword would be the best against a dragon. Cheryl was about to climb up the wall by the time Lucca, Vivi, and I had our weapons. She opted for carrying none. She never liked blades.

"How are we going to do this? You only have two hands, Vivi," Cheryl points out.

"Someone will have to ride piggyback." She smirks at Lucca.

He rewards her with a droll stare. "Do you think that bothers me?"

Lucca gets behind her and then jumps on her back. Her balance is barely altered. Now that she's recovered her powers, she's as strong as the rest of us.

Cheryl and I stand on each side of her. She takes our hands and then asks, "Ready?"

When we all confirm, she takes off. My stomach drops as the feeling of free-falling hits me. Then it's like I'm stuck on a roller coaster, traveling at the speed of light. For a moment, I lose the sensation of my body, and it's terrifying. I'm not sure how long it takes, but when our speed returns to normal, my heart is about to somersault out of my chest.

"For fuck's sake." I press my hand over my racing heart.

"That was awesome!" Lucca says, then places a kiss on Vivi's neck before jumping off her back.

I stare at Cheryl and notice her face is a little paler. I'm glad I wasn't the only one who experienced something other than a thrill. She doesn't say anything though as she steps away, her attention on the towering mountain in front of us. We never came this close to the place on that evening so many centuries ago.

"How are we getting up to the top?" she asks.

"I tried to walk the wind there, but there's a barrier even I couldn't breach," Vivi answers.

"Fuck. Don't tell me we need to climb the mountain?" Lucca asks.

"No. There's an entrance somewhere nearby. It's concealed by powerful magic though."

"Can you find it?" I ask.

Vivi nods. "I believe so."

A terrifying roar comes from the top of the mountain, making the small hairs on the back of my neck stand on end.

"What the hell was that?" I pull my sword from its sheath, glad we came prepared.

"I think... I think it was the Elder dragon," Vivi replies.

Cheryl gasps. "Karl."

Twenty-Five

KARL

ITALY, 1520

At first, I don't know where I am. The last memory I have is of fighting Dietrich and spilling his blood on the cold, snowy ground. I'm lying in front of a fireplace that still burns, and an animal pelt covers the lower half of my body. I've shifted back to my human form. My wounds have been healed, but my body is still sore.

I turn around and find Manu sleeping next to me. Unlike me, she's fully dressed, and the bloodstains on her tunic tell me all she did was remove her armor before she fell asleep. I reach out and touch her beautiful face. Love and admiration swell in my heart, filling my chest.

She blinks her eyes open and then smiles softly. "You're awake."

"Yes. What happened?"

"You don't remember anything?"

"I remember killing Dietrich."

Her eyebrows furrow. "You don't remember the Nightingale priest or what he did?"

I read anguish in her eyes, and that troubles me. I cup her

cheek, and the moment I touch her, all the memories that followed Dietrich's fall rush by and flood my brain.

"I'm your familiar."

She nods. "You don't regret it, do you? The priest said you had agreed to it. He read your mind. It was the only way to save you."

A tear rolls down her face, and it confirms how much this is weighing on her.

"I don't regret it, my love. You're my mate. I'd follow you to the bowels of hell."

I bring her face to mine and cover her sweet lips with my own. They part, allowing me to deepen the kiss. The mating bond explodes in my veins, but it's heightened by a new power. The familiar bond. It makes what I feel stronger, and the need to protect Manu at all costs is not only a necessity but also a vow I intend to keep, no matter the cost.

The need to claim her, to brand her body with mine, is all I can think of now. I roll on top of her, spreading her legs. She lets out a throaty moan when I press my erection against her heat. I let go of her mouth to kiss her jaw, neck, and everything else on the path down to her pussy. Her fingers curl around my hair, and when I capture her nipple between my teeth, she yanks a strand hard.

"Karl... please."

I let go of her breast and look at her. Her fangs are on full display. I look forward to another one of her love bites, but first I need to satiate another hunger.

"Please what, darling?"

"I need to feel you inside me."

"Soon enough, love."

I lick her stomach all the way down to her pelvis, pleased with myself when her skin breaks out in goose bumps. Her fingers have released my hair to curl around the blanket underneath us. I place open kisses above her sex while I tease her entrance with my fingers. She cries out when I slide my thumb over her nub. I repeat the movement a couple of times before temptation becomes too much and only tasting her on my tongue will suffice.

I lick her bundle of nerves from top to bottom, then sideways. With each stroke of my tongue, Manu's cries become louder. It's getting harder and harder for me not to empty myself on the blanket instead of inside her. My balls are tight, ready to explode, but I want to taste her as she comes, so I keep licking and sucking, ignoring her pleas to fuck her with my cock.

I'm deep in her folds when she screams my name at the top of her lungs. Her body trembles under me, but I keep feasting until I have my fill. Only when she relaxes and stops moving do I slide back up.

Her eyes are half closed, and her lips are parted. "You're the devil, Karl."

I smile. "No, I'm a wolf. A hungry wolf."

"I thought you ate plenty."

"Not nearly enough."

I lean back and lift one of her legs, placing it over my shoulder. Her glistening sex opens up for me, ready and waiting.

"I want to take you hard, Princess. No, I *need* to take you hard."

"I'm yours to do with as you please."

Fuck me. If that doesn't make me almost come right here and now. I've never heard anything more alluring in my life.

With a precise push, I sheathe myself in her. It's like coming home. She gasps and then tightens her walls around me. The wicked upcurl of her lips tells me she's challenging me.

I pull back and slam into her again, harder this time. She moans, closing her eyes for a moment. A hazy fog of desire surrounds me, and then comes the frenzy. My pace increases as I chase the blissful moment when I fall apart in her arms. I never knew being mated to someone would feel like this. It's a sensation that goes beyond myself. It wraps around Manu, connecting us on a level deeper than pure carnal desire. She's everything to me. The entire universe.

My thoughts are scattered just like all the stars in the sky. I try to postpone my release for as long as I can, but my body has a will of its own. I explode inside her, pumping in and out faster and faster. My pulse is pounding in my ears, but I can still hear the sound of my ragged breathing.

Without stopping, I pull Manu to a sitting position so I can kiss her again. Her leg slides off my shoulder to curl around my hip. She's moving now too, prolonging my orgasm. I know exactly what she needs because I need it too. I release her lips and offer her my neck. The sweet bite comes swiftly, and as she drinks from me, I come again.

Her body tenses right before she climaxes as well. This is probably what heaven feels like, and I get to live it with Manu every day forever.

We tumble sideways on the blanket, legs and arms twisted together, and let oblivion take us over.

RONAN

I shouldn't go check on Cheryl, but I can't help myself when it comes to her. If she were a witch, I'd believe she put a spell on me.

She's not in the quarters the king assigned to her, so I follow her scent until I reach the gardens near the first wall.

I don't have a visual of her at first, as she's concealed by a giant potted plant, but I can hear her crying. Hell, I don't know if I should stay or leave.

"I know you're there, bloodsucker," she says.

Of course she does. She's a wolf, after all.

"I came to check on you."

"You came to check on me or make me more miserable?"

I walk over to her hiding spot before I answer her. She's sitting against the giant vase, hugging her legs. Her chin is propped on her knees, and by the way her eyes are red and her cheeks are wet, I can guess she's been crying for a while.

"What's wrong?"

She wipes her face and looks up to glare. It's her default expression when it comes to me.

"You wouldn't understand."

I crouch so we're on the same level. "Try me."

"Now that Karl is his mate's familiar, he'll live forever."

"And that's a bad thing?"

She looks away. "I knew you wouldn't understand."

"Why don't you explain it to me as if I were five, then?"

She makes a sound that sounds a lot like a laugh, but her sour-puss expression contradicts the noise.

"You probably have the maturity of a five-year-old despite your old age."

"How old do you think I am?"

She shrugs. "I don't know. Over a hundred?"

I shake my head, laughing. "I was born in 1495."

Her eyebrows arch. "You're only four years older than Karl, then. Still, I maintain you're as immature as a child."

I sigh. "I'm trying to help here. You're not making it easy. For better or for worse, you're part of the king's inner circle. We should get along."

"I have no one else in this world. Karl is all I have left, but he's now bound to your precious princess in the worst way possible."

"You truly believe becoming a familiar is that bad?"

"Yes!" she exclaims, throwing her hands in the air. "Like I said, you're a vampire. How could you understand?"

"You think familiars are what? Slaves?"

"I don't know what to think. It's all fine and good for an animal to become a familiar. It's like they're upgraded. But Karl was a wolf shifter, and now he's less."

I shake my head. "He's not less. I think it's about time you start looking at the big picture."

"I see the big picture. He's nothing without her. His life is bound to hers. If she dies in the war, he dies. How is that fair?"

"Life is not fair, Cheryl. If it were, you wouldn't have been betrayed by your family. I wouldn't have lost mine when I was too young to pick up a sword."

She pauses at that. "You're an orphan too?"

I nod.

"I'm sorry," she says in a low whisper.

"It happened a long time ago. I barely remember them."

"That's my biggest fear. Eventually I'll die, either cut by a blade or of old age. Karl will live on. As the years go by, he won't remember what I look like, the sound of my voice. I'll be nothing, not even dust in the wind."

"Is that what you're most afraid of? To be forgotten?"

"Yes."

"I won't forget you."

The words leave my mouth before I can stop them, and I curse in my head.

"Don't say that only to make me feel better. You just confessed that you can barely remember your own family, and they haven't been dead for that long."

"I'm not saying that to mollify you."

I rise from my crouch. I've said enough, and if I stay here, I might confess things I'm not ready to contemplate yet.

Twenty-Six

KARL

INDIGO MOUNTAIN, PRESENT DAY

Ryker drops us off by the foot of Indigo Mountain and disappears in the next second without even a farewell. It's up to Solomon to guide us the rest of the way, and he does so while muttering curses under his breath.

"So, where exactly does the Elder dragon live?" Vaughn asks.

"At the top of the mountain, naturally," Solomon replies.

"Fuck me. Please tell me we don't have to climb the mountain. I'm getting dizzy just looking at it."

"There's another way. We can reach the top from inside, but I'm afraid not climbing anything is not possible, unless you can fly."

I'm glad we don't have to pretend to be Alex Honnold, the famous rock climber. Wolves are not fans of heights, and I'm not an exception.

A growl nearby makes me jump on the spot. Vaughn steps closer to me, body coiled with tension.

"What was that?" he asks.

"Who knows? Let's not wait here to find out," Solomon says.

"Where's the entrance? I hope it's not far."

There's fear in his voice, and I regret bringing him on this trip. I forgot Vaughn would get spooked by just about anything. He couldn't even watch horror movies with us without covering his eyes for eighty percent of the time.

"It's on the other side of that boulder." Solomon points. "Come on."

I follow him but keep my eyes peeled and my ears open for any sign of danger. When we round the boulder, there's nothing but a smooth wall.

"I don't see any entrance." Vaughn makes that helpful observation.

Solomon looks over his shoulder, sporting a glint that says he thinks little of the vampire. "It's concealed. Do you think the Elder dragon wants any idiot stumbling upon her lair?"

"I assume you know the spell to reveal the entrance to us," I say.

The dry crack of a twig breaking sounds nearby. We are not alone.

"What are you waiting for? For the monster prowling to attack us?" Vaughn complains.

Solomon wastes precious seconds glaring at him before he faces the mountain and begins to recite a spell in a language I don't recognize. The rocky wall in front of us vibrates and then caves inward, revealing a dark passage.

"Voilà." Solomon makes a grand gesture with his arm. "You can go first, Vaughn, since you're so afraid of monsters."

He doesn't move, just stands there staring at the black void.

"I'll go first," I say and stride forward.

No sooner than Vaughn and Solomon are inside the tunnel, the wall solidifies again.

"I hope the spell to open that is the same," Vaughn mutters.

"Stop bitching and move," Solomon barks. "Manu is still trapped in Ellnesari, and we don't know how long it will take to convince the Elder dragon to part with the mirror. You know how dragons love their treasures."

He doesn't need to remind me that we're operating on borrowed time. I just hope—no, I pray that Manu doesn't get herself killed. It's not that I'm afraid of dying. I just don't want to depart this world before I know why she hurt me so much.

My eyesight has adjusted to the gloom. It's not completely dark inside the mountain. There's light coming from fissures on the ceiling, but I don't know if they're magical or natural. At the end of the tunnel, I see the beginning of stairs.

"How many steps do you reckon until we get to the top?" Vaughn asks.

"No idea. Why don't you count?" I joke.

It takes us at least an hour to reach the top of the mountain, and by then my legs are on the verge of folding onto themselves.

Vaughn crawls over the last steps, panting. "Jesus fucking Christ. I think climbing the mountain from outside would have been easier."

"Pathetic." Solomon steps over him, looking fresh as hell.

"How are you not tired?" I ask as I massage my legs.

"I suppose I'm built of better stuff than you lot."

"Pishposh," a voice echoes in the large chamber before us. The ground trembles with the noise.

Damn. That must be the Elder dragon.

Vaughn staggers back to his feet and stares ahead.

"You're not built of better stuff, Corvicus. You just know more spells."

The Elder dragon finally steps from under the shadows to stand right beneath the moonlight coming from the opening at the top of the humongous room.

From the corner of my eye, I see Vaughn doing the sign of the cross. As if that's going to protect him against the three-headed beast staring at us. She's more terrifying than I imagined, but also magnificent. Her scales are silver and shimmer under the moonlight.

"My, my, my. I never thought I'd see your face again," the head in the middle says, staring at Solomon.

"Trust me, I had no desire to ever come here again, but I had no choice."

The dragon switches her attention to Vaughn and me, using her left and right heads to do so. "Oh, you brought me gifts?"

Vaughn looks at me, all panicked and shit. I shake my head, trying to signal for him to calm the fuck down.

"A vampire and the wolf shifter familiar. Interesting," the head in the middle says.

The head closest to Vaughn takes a whiff of him. "This one was turned recently."

"As I had foreseen," the head on the left pipes up.

"What do you want, Corvicus?" the middle head says. She seems to be the one in charge here.

"I came for the Nightingale mirror," Solomon replies.

The heads rear back and then glance at one another. A second later, all three laugh loudly.

That doesn't bode well.

"You're a comedian, Corvicus," the middle head says.

"He's not joking. We don't want to keep the mirror. We just want to use it to open a portal into Ellnesari," I say.

"The portals have been closed for a reason, boy. Do not open that can of worms again."

"I need to return. It's a life-and-death situation," I grit out.

"Oh, I see great pain in your past," the head on the right says.

"And more pain in your future," the left head adds.

I throw my hands in the air. "Great. I'm cursed to suffer forever. I still need the mirror."

"And what would you give us in return for it?" the head in the middle asks.

"What do you want?"

"Foolish boy. Don't ask them what they want," Solomon chimes in, but I ignore him.

"Hmmm. We haven't had company in a very long time. How about we play a little game?" the middle head asks.

"Oh no, no, no." Solomon steps in front of me, shaking his

head and wagging his finger. "We're not doing this again. That's how I lost the mirror to you in the first place."

"We do not wish to play with you, old fool." The head in the middle glowers at him.

"Besides, it's not your decision," the head closest to me adds.

"That's right, it's my decision," I say. "We don't have time for games."

"But we like to play games. We rarely have company."

"I could sing," Vaughn suggests.

The Elder dragon seems intrigued at first, but suddenly she stands at her full height, and then the head in the middle lets out a piercing roar that makes the walls tremble and the ground shake. Bits of rock detach from the ceiling and rain down on us.

Hell, she's going to make this cave collapse.

"I think she really hates that idea," I tell Vaughn.

"She isn't mad at you. Something ticked her off," Solomon explains, then furrows his brows. "Ah hell. Those stupid fools. I told them not to come."

"Who came?"

Solomon looks at me. "It seems your friend Vivienne decided to crash this party. And she brought company."

"Who?"

"Your sister."

Twenty-Seven

RONAN

ITALY, 1521

"Hold your form, Cheryl," I yell as she barely manages to block Lucca's attack.

"I'm trying," she grits out.

Lucca jumps back and begins to circle her once more. "Come on, Cher. You can do better than this."

"Quit calling me Cher," she snarls, and her eyes flash yellow.

"You'd better put your wolf on a leash. She's going to pounce." Dean laughs.

She whips her face to him, and everything in her body tells me she's about to shift and indeed pounce on Dean. I step into the training circle, blocking Cheryl's view from him.

"We're done for today," I say.

"Why? I'm not tired."

"Well, I am. And I'm also hungry. I haven't fed yet."

She twists her face into a scowl. "Please do not remind me of your disgusting eating habits."

"How is it different than when you hunt in wolf form?" Lucca asks.

"I only eat in my wolf form out of necessity. Stop holding that one incident over my head."

"I will never stop, and you know why?"

She narrows her eyes. "Because you're an ass?"

"No, because it bothers you when I tease." He winks and then heads to the wall to hang his training sword.

"I think I'm going to the feeding room as well," Dean declares. "Training has whetted up my appetite." He flexes his arms, showing off for Cheryl.

It didn't take long for him to forget that Cheryl took a bite out of his arm and almost killed him once he noticed how gorgeous she is. Now he alternates between teasing her and following her everywhere like a lovesick puppy, a fact that pisses me off more than it should.

As for my relationship with her, there have been some improvements. She lets me train her in sword combat without biting my head off, but she still doesn't trust me. In fact, she's not close to anyone here save her brother.

But as a mated wolf, he spends most of his time with Manu, which means Cheryl is most often alone or in her wolf form. I wish she'd let someone in. Manu has tried, and Lucca as well. But if I'm being honest with myself, I'd hoped she'd open up to me after our conversation in the gardens last year.

The soldiers and guards were ordered to not bother our resident wolves, but they still keep a close watch on them, especially on Cheryl.

"You call having your ass handed to you training?" Cheryl teases, bringing me back to the here and now.

"I did better than you," he retorts.

"But I'm a wolf. I can kill without a sword."

Dean runs his hand over the scar on his arm. "Yes, I remember."

Sullen now, he walks out of the room without glancing back.

"You shouldn't have said that," Lucca tells her.

Cheryl scoffs. "Someone has to tell him the truth. He's the worst trainee in the program."

"He wasn't that bad until you started training with us."

I give Lucca a warning stare, but he's not looking at me.

"Are you saying it's my fault Dean underperforms? That's ludicrous."

"He's infatuated with you," he deadpans, then smirks.

I want to punch that smugness off his face. What is he trying to accomplish by telling Cheryl that?

Her surprise morphs into something that resembles pity. It makes me feel better even though it's an awful sentiment. I'm jealous of a sixteen-year-old male. It's pathetic.

"That's unfortunate. Vampires aren't my type."

She locks her eyes with mine for a moment, almost as if she wants me to get that notion into my head. I probably should. There's no time in war for unrequited love. But it's a fact that I haven't been able to fuck anyone since she moved into the fortress.

"So you plan on remaining single for the rest of your life? There aren't any wolf shifters nearby," Lucca points out.

She shrugs. "I don't mind humans. At least I can expect them to live as long as me."

Her expression closes off, but her words keep ringing in my head even after she walks out of the room.

I don't notice Lucca has come to stand at my side until he speaks again. "You too, huh?"

"What are you talking about?"

"Don't play dumb with me. I see how you look at Cheryl. You want her."

I turn my back to him because I don't trust my face to not reveal the truth.

"You don't know anything, Luc. And if you keep saying shit like that, folks might confuse you for an old busybody."

"I hope you like your stay in denial land. But don't entertain the idea further. Cheryl is mortal. There's no future in a relationship with her, and I know you wouldn't dare go after her only for a quick tumble in the haystack."

Hearing him say that about me also eats me alive. Guilt turns my body to stone. That's what I did last year with Manu. I fucked her, took away her virginity, only to then erect a wall between us. I acted like a cad, but I can't ever tell Lucca the truth.

"I don't want any relationship with her. Stop seeing things that aren't there."

"I have to tell you something my uncle told me in confidence."

I glance at him with my eyebrows furrowed. "If he told you in confidence, then you shouldn't tell me anything."

"I planned to keep his secret, but I think it will benefit you to know. Cheryl requested an audience with him and my mother a few days ago."

Lucca's somber tone matches his expression. He earns my undivided attention.

"What for? Does she plan to leave the fortress?"

"No. She asked if it was possible for a wolf shifter to be turned into a vampire."

My eyes widen. "She wants to be turned? But she hates our kind."

"I'm beginning to believe she doesn't hate us. She's just using us as a target for all the shit that's happened to her. Her parents are dead, and the asshole wolf who betrayed them as well. She has nowhere to aim her anger besides at us."

I rub my face and look ahead, seeing nothing. "What did the king say?"

"He said it wasn't possible."

"He's certain of it?"

Lucca shakes his head. "No, he's not certain. He lied to her."

"Why would he li... oh. He doesn't want her to ask anyone here to turn her because he doesn't know what will happen."

He nods. "Precisely. We have too many problems on our hands with Tatiana and the war. The last thing we need is a mutant on top of everything else."

"If she's determined about becoming an immortal, she'll look for answers elsewhere."

"She could become a familiar. Maybe yours." He smirks.

I narrow my eyes. "I don't want a familiar. And you know her view on the matter."

That wipes the grin right off his face. "Yeah, I know. Shall we head for the feeding room, then? I'm famished."

"I think I need a hot bath more than I need food. I'll meet you later."

"More for me, then."

On my way to my quarters, I pick up Cheryl's scent. I should let her be, but there's something strange about the smell, almost as if it was corrupted. *Damn it. What now?* I follow the scent on quick feet until I turn a corner and find her bracing against the wall, clutching her middle.

"Cheryl, what happened?" I try to help her, but she pushes me back.

"Nothing happened, Ronan. Mind your own business."

Her long hair hides part of her face, but she won't meet my gaze anyway.

"Look at me."

She turns around, flattening her back against the stone wall. Her skin is covered in sweat, and she seems to be in great pain. "What?"

"Something happened to you. Why are you holding yourself like that? Did Lucca strike you too hard?"

"He didn't."

"Regardless, I'm taking you to see the healer." I take her arm, but she struggles against my hold.

"I don't need a healer, you idiot. What ails me is self-inflicted."

"What are you saying?"

"I took wolfsbane," she grits out.

"You did what?" I let go of her arm.

"You heard me."

"What for? Are you insane?"

"I've been taking small doses every day to build my resistance against the poison. It's the only way to become immune to it."

"It's clearly not working."

"I miscalculated the dosage today and took a little too much."

"You need the antidote."

"No! If I take the antidote now, all my effort will have been for nothing. I'll have to start again."

"So what do you plan to do? Crawl your way back to your chambers?"

"Hopefully it won't come to crawling. Maybe slinking."

"Don't be ridiculous. I'll help you to your room."

She sighs. "Fine, but don't you dare pick me up in your arms."

It had crossed my mind, but it's better if I don't get too close to her. Wicked thoughts fill my head when I do.

She leans against my side, and slowly we make our way back to the main corridor.

"How bad are the side effects when you take wolfsbane in small portions?" I ask.

"The first time it was horrible. I couldn't move for most of the evening. I just stared at the ceiling and thought about my favorite fables."

"You couldn't sleep?"

"One of the effects of wolfsbane is lethargy, hence why I had to fight the throes of slumber."

"Hmmm."

She snorts. "That's the best reply I've ever received from you."

"Why is that?"

"It doesn't have a condescending tone."

We arrive at her door, but she doesn't make a motion to open it. I glance at her face and see she's struggling to lift her arm.

"I can he—"

"No, let me try. You won't be there the next time someone poisons me with wolfsbane. I need to fight the drug on my own."

Of course, *I* was the person who poisoned her last. But she didn't bring it up, so I'll keep my mouth shut.

Finally she lifts her arm and yanks at the skeleton key hanging on a cord from her neck. Inserting the key in the hole is another story. Her hand won't stop shaking.

I cover her hand with mine. "Let me help you, please. Standing here all night instead of resting won't do you any good."

Surprisingly, she lets me guide her hand and then turn the key. I wouldn't dream of doing everything on my own. I understand that she needs to maintain control over what her body does.

Her chambers are small, much smaller than mine, and there's no receiving room, so we walk straight into her bedroom. I avoid looking at her bed and focus on the fireplace that, at the moment, is cold and gray.

"It's freezing in here. I'll light a fire. Where would you like to sit?" I ask.

"Bed. I need to lie down."

I help her to it, and when she doesn't send me away immediately, I cover her with a blanket and then watch her curl underneath it. Her eyes connect with mine, and it's like she's reeling me into their depths.

"Thank you, Ronan."

I don't move. I can't breathe. I can only stare at her like an idiot while my heart gallops at full speed.

"What?" she asks.

"It's the first time you've thanked me and actually meant it."

The corners of her lips curl into a faint smile. "What can I say? You grew on me."

Not only does my heart feel like it's going to jump out of my chest, but I also get a strange feeling in the pit of my stomach.

This is madness. I can't indulge in emotions that could compromise my position in King Raphael's court, especially when she's asking around about becoming a vampire.

"Ronan? How about that fire?"

I shake my head to try to get some sense in it. "I'm on it."

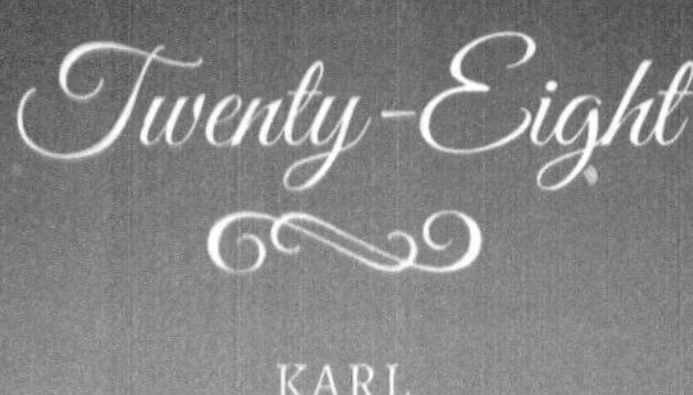

KARL

INDIGO MOUNTAIN, PRESENT DAY

None of us breathe as we wait for the dragon's next move. She unfolds her wings and then launches into the air. A second later, she's gone.

"Fuck, she's going after Cheryl," I exclaim. "We need to stop her."

I turn around, ready to dash down the stairs, when Solomon grabs my arm and stops me.

"Don't be stupid, Karl. We came for the mirror. Let's find it first."

"You want to steal the mirror from that beast?" Vaughn asks in a high-pitched voice.

"Would you rather wait for the Elder dragon to return and beg for it?" Solomon snaps. "She likes to toy with people. She'll never let you have the mirror. Ryker said we needed a miracle to retrieve the object. This is our miracle."

Damn it. He's right. I have to hope Vivi and Cheryl can handle the dragon until we get what we came for.

Now that she's gone, I can see what her huge body was

hiding. Spread throughout the chamber are several mountains of treasure. Gold objects and jewels sparkle under the moonlight.

"Where do we begin to look?" I ask.

"Let me handle the search, boy."

Solomon closes his eyes and stretches his hands forward while he recites a spell in an unknown language.

The shiny objects that are piled in several mounds start to vibrate and make a hell of a lot of noise. Solomon continues, his voice growing louder and louder as he goes.

"I don't like the looks of this," Vaughn mutters under his breath. "Doesn't it seem like those mountains of treasure are about to explode?"

A second later, that's exactly what happens to one. I push him down as I drop to the floor and then cover my head. I wait for us to be buried under the Elder's dragon trove, but not a single object falls on us. The noise they make as they land on the ground is deafening, though, and it seems to echo endlessly.

Finally, when the chamber is quiet again, I uncover my head and lean up on my elbows. Solomon is standing in front of us, holding the small mirror in his hand and smiling.

"Got it. Now let's get those fools before the dragon turns them into ashes."

CHERYL

No sooner do we hear the roar of a dragon than the beast erupts from the top of the mountain in all her three-headed glory. She's bigger than a freaking airplane, and I gawk at her with my mouth open.

"Hell, how do we fight that?" Lucca asks.

"Definitely not with your puny swords," I say.

"Or your sharp teeth," Ronan adds.

"Go find Karl and the others. I'll distract her," Vivi commands as she steps forward.

"Are you mad? I'm not going to let you fight a dragon alone," Lucca retorts.

She looks at him without a hint of worry on her face. "I'll be fine, Luc."

The dragon roars, the sound amplified when it comes from three heads. Vivi begins to move her arms as if she were a dancer. Wind gathers around her, making her long hair flap around her head. She keeps building her powers as the dragon dives for her.

Shit, and none of us are moving.

"Come on, let's go!" I take off, giving Vivi a wide berth as I run for the cover of trees.

I know Ronan followed me, but Lucca, the stubborn male he is, remains by his girlfriend's side. Oh well. I can't fault him for that. Love does make us do crazy things.

The roaring and flapping of the Elder dragon's wings grows louder as she comes closer. I dare to look over my shoulder and regret it. Vivi and Lucca look like tiny insects who are about to be crushed by a monster. Ronan's attention is also diverted to the scene.

When the middle head of the dragon opens her mouth and the glow of fire appears from the depths of her throat, Vivi uses all the power she gathered around her to shove the dragon backward until she disappears in the midnight sky.

I stop running. "Holy crap. I didn't know Vivi was that powerful."

By the way Lucca is staring at her, he didn't either. But when Vivi collapses to her knees, he's there to pick her up.

"Should we go help them?" I ask.

"No. They're fine," Ronan insists. "Keep going toward the mountain. Vivi bought us some time. Let's not waste it."

"We don't know where the secret entrance to the mountain is," I say. "Only Vivi can find it."

Ronan curses under his breath. "Right. I forgot about that part."

"They're coming," I tell him.

Lucca is helping Vivi walk, and when they're near, I can see her face is a little gray.

"Are you okay?" I ask softly.

She turns to me. "I'll be fine in a minute. It's been a while since I used my powers like that. I'm a little rusty."

"A little rusty? You blew a three-headed dragon into space."

Ronan looks up. "Not quite into space. She's coming back, and I bet a million bucks she's mad as hell now."

I squint at the sky and see a dark shadow that's growing larger. We might have a few minutes before the dragon is back.

"I don't think I can pull that stunt again," Vivi says.

"Can you find the entrance to her lair?" My voice rises a little. It's getting harder and harder to keep calm.

"We can't hope to go inside, find Karl, and run away before she returns," Ronan replies.

"You won't need to," Karl says from nearby, making my heart soar with relief.

I turn around in a flash and see him striding toward us, with Vaughn and Solomon in tow. I break into a run and crush him in a hug.

"You're okay," I exclaim. "I was so worried about you."

"I'm fine, Cheryl. But what are you doing here?"

"I came to help you."

"And help you did, girl." Solomon smiles. It's an odd sight.

"Did you recover the mirror?" Ronan asks.

He pulls the small object from inside his shirt. "I sure did. Thanks to your distraction."

My back tenses suddenly, the sign that danger is fast approaching. I look at the sky and confirm the Elder dragon is much closer to us now.

"We need to leave."

"I can't walk the wind with all of you at once," Vivi says, desperation lacing her words.

"Can you use the mirror to open a portal for us?" Karl asks.

"I don't know."

"You have to try or we're all doomed," Ronan says.

"Stop putting pressure on her!" Lucca pulls her closer to him. His eyes flash red, and he's clearly showing off his fangs in an aggressive manner.

"Calm down," I say.

"Hand over the mirror." Vivi holds out her hand.

"Here. I'll ground you," Solomon says, "and feed you my power if needed."

"Guys, the Elder dragon is getting closer," Vaughn warns us.

I look up and realize our time has run out. The dragon is almost within striking distance. This is quickly turning into a mission impossible.

Suddenly, I see a dark shadow approach from the east.

"Another dragon is coming," I tell everyone.

Vaughn pulls his hair back, yanking at the strands. "Fucking hell. We're dead."

Ronan steps forward, squinting. "I think I know that dragon."

"Great. Maybe you can sit down and have tea with it," Vaughn grumbles.

Ignoring Vaughn, I pay close attention to the winged beast flying as fast as a jet plane. Only one dragon that size can move that fast: the king. I've only seen him in his dragon form once, but it made an impression on me.

"Holy crap. That's Larsson," I say.

"Hell, what is he doing here?" Lucca asks.

Larsson zooms across the sky, which is already turning lighter. Sunrise is maybe an hour away. We either travel to Ellnesari or we need to find cover soon.

"Apparently, he's stopping the Elder dragon from killing us," Vaughn replies.

"Forget the dragons," Solomon snaps. "Vivi, I need you to concentrate on where you want the portal to open."

"But I don't know the spell," she whines.

"And won't we need a ritual like last time?" I ask, then realize that with Vivi occupied with the mirror, the only female who can participate is me.

My eyes connect with Ronan's, and I know he just came to the same conclusion. My face warms when he doesn't look away. We've crossed that line before, and it almost destroyed me. I don't think I can go through the pain of his rejection again.

"This isn't like the Taluah Mirror, which was used for many things and required more magic in order to work as a portal creator," Solomon explains. "This is the Kashir mirror. Its sole purpose was to allow people to see their destinations before they arrived."

"So not to open portals, then," I say.

"Correct. However, I was able to make some tweaks and change its setting, per se."

"You modified one of our relics?" Vivi asks. "How did you have the knowledge to do so?"

"Ah, that's a story for another time. Let's try to get you lot to Ellnesari before something else happens."

"You knew this mirror could open a portal into Ellnesari and you didn't think to tell us until now?" Lucca asks, clearly annoyed with the familiar.

Solomon returns the glare. "The mirror couldn't do that without Nightingale magic, and we didn't have that at our disposal the last time."

"What do I need to do?" Vivi asks, getting us back on track.

"Like I said, look into the mirror and picture the location where you want to go. Ideally, somewhere in Ellnesari that's safe."

"I don't know where is safe and where isn't anymore. I definitely can't get inside the palace. It's protected by heavy wards."

"We should cross into where we last saw Manu," Karl chimes in. "It'll be impossible to track her otherwise."

His answer doesn't make Vivi happy. Her eyebrows furrow together, and her lips turn into a thin flat line.

"We were in the Hornet's Gardens. Hardly the safest palace in the Kingdom of Aquila."

"We don't have a choice," he insists.

She takes a deep breath. "I know."

She diverts her attention to the small mirror in her hands, and soon her eyes become unfocused. I can't see the magic at work, but I can definitely sense it. It's powerful and seems to reverberate inside my chest.

Without any prompt from Solomon, she begins to recite a spell in a foreign language. Her eyes change from blue to silver, and then her entire body glows from within. It's a freaky sight.

A gust of wind comes from behind me, and I fear it's one of the dragons sweeping down to obliterate us. I turn, bracing for the strike, but it's neither Larsson nor the Elder dragon. It's a portal that Vivi just managed to open using the mirror.

In the case of the Taluah Mirror, the object itself became a gateway, but I suppose we wouldn't be able to squeeze through such a small opening.

"Vivi, you did it," Karl says.

He doesn't wait for any of us before he steps into the light and vanishes from sight.

"Karl, wait, damn it." I run after him, and immediately I know the portal is already getting smaller.

A rush of magic covers my body, and it feels like my skin is getting pricked by a thousand needles. I want to scream, but there's no sound in the white void. A warm hand on my back tells me I'm not alone. I don't need to turn to know it's Ronan traveling with me.

We land hard on the ground, his body half covering mine. For a moment, neither of us moves. I don't know about him, but my ears are ringing, and my body feels numb, a sensation not different from when wolfsbane is in my system. I tense as the memories of being helpless flood my brain.

Ronan's arm tightens around me. "It's okay, Cher. You're fine," he whispers in my ear.

His warm breath fans over my skin, and I stop breathing for a second. I close my eyes, not wanting to see the look in his. All the feelings I've suppressed for all these years return with a vengeance. I love this male with all my heart, and he doesn't even know.

No. I will not become that stupid mess again.

"Let me go, Ronan." I shove him off me.

He rolls off to the side and then jumps to his feet. My body is no longer numb, so I follow his example, refusing to look at him now. My heart is beating faster, a reaction to his embrace, and I hate that he can hear it.

"Where's your brother?" he asks.

"I'm here." Karl steps out from behind a bush.

I don't like the look on his face.

"Did you pick up Manu's scent?" I ask.

"I did."

"What's wrong, then?"

He rubs his chin and looks off in the distance. "I also picked up another scent. She wasn't alone."

"Do you think she was captured?" Ronan asks.

"We're in Ellnesari, and she's a vampire who shouldn't be here. The odds are that's what happened."

"Stupid cow," I mutter under my breath.

There was a time that I thought Manu and I could have been friends. That was before she betrayed Karl. If his life wasn't bound to hers, I'd have killed that bitch by now. I've never hated anyone as much as I hate her. She surpassed Dietrich's treachery by a mile.

"There's no point in calling her names. We have to find her," Karl says, then looks over my head. "Wait. Where are the others?"

"The portal lost its mojo fast. We barely made it through," Ronan replies.

Karl doesn't say anything for a couple of beats, but the deep *V* between his eyebrows tells me his brain is working furiously.

"Better this way," he finally says. "The fewer people in our party, the less chance will be discovered."

I cross my arms, hating his logic. "I don't agree with that. It'd be nice to have a Nightingale in our party."

"We don't, so we'll have to make do without them," Ronan grumbles. "Karl, lead the way."

Twenty-Nine

MANU

I ignore the tightness in my chest as I run away from the portal. Guilt is a terrible thing, but I couldn't return to Salem and a life of eternal misery. This is my only chance to break the curse. I can't go on as I have for the last five hundred years.

Everyone believes I'm bitter because of the way I look. No one knows that's not the worst part of my punishment. To look at Karl, to see the hurt in his eyes and not be able to tell him why I had to push him away is pure agony.

My heart is beating too fast; my pulse is pounding in my ears. I'm all too aware of the dangers of staying behind. My chances of success are slim, and yet here I am. I'm either the stupidest person on the planet or the most hopeful.

The buzzing of giant wings flapping nearby makes my heart skip a beat. Vivi's father warned us about the creatures that live here. In theory, my attire should protect me from them, but I trust the Nightingales as far as I can throw them.

I run faster. Desperation begins to spread in my heart like a disease. No, I can't let the sentiment take control. I need to remember why I'm doing this. It's for Karl, for the life that was stolen from us.

The mantra doesn't work fast enough. I realize I'm not alone anymore, only a second before I'm hit by a paralyzing spell. I can't make my legs work, but I still have the momentum of my run, which sends me careening to the ground face-first. Dirt fills my mouth, making me gag.

"You were ordered to leave," a male says.

At first, I can only see his boots, but when I look up, I recognize his face. He's one of the soldiers reporting to the queen. I believe Telar is his name. His cold expression tells me I'm not going to find an ally in him. *Shit.*

He pulls me up and then, to my surprise, releases me.

"Why are you still here?" he asks, watching me as if I were a bug.

I have to spit the dirt from my mouth before I can say, "None of your business."

His expression twists into one of disgust. "You bloodsuckers are not only savages, but you're also as dumb as rocks."

"Fuck you."

Rage shines in his eyes, and I expect a blow any second. But all he does is clench his jaw hard until I can hear his molars grind. He must be under orders to not harm me, because I read clearly in his eyes that he very much wants to punch me.

I tense my legs and prepare to run, but they don't move. The asshole notices my intention and smirks.

"Don't bother. You're not going anywhere unless I allow it." He pulls out a long vine that was wrapped around his belt and binds my hands together. They glow when they're tight.

"Am I your prisoner now?"

"Yes. Now move." He shoves me forward.

The buzzing I heard earlier becomes louder. I look at the sky, but I can't see what's making that noise through the thick cover of the forest canopy.

"Shouldn't we look for cover?"

He shakes his head. "You defied the king's orders and stayed, and now you're concerned about some measly insects?"

I mutter several choice words under my breath and stay put. If he wants me to move, he'll have to drag me.

Unfazed, he walks ahead and doesn't look back. I soon discover why. I'm yanked forward as if there were a cord connecting me to him. It must be these damn golden vines around my wrists.

"Where are you taking me?"

He doesn't answer.

"What's the matter? Did the cat catch your tongue?"

I hurry forward and then bend over to pick up a rock I see on my path.

"Hey, I'm talking to you." I throw the rock, hitting him on the back of his head.

He stops, then turns around slowly. The hatred shining in his eyes should terrify me, but I can work with that. I've had years of practice.

He walks over, projecting a menacing stance that I'm sure works well for him on the battlefield. I lift my chin in defiance.

"You're lucky that I'm under strict orders not to harm you," he sneers.

"Oh yeah? Whose orders? That bitch queen of yours?"

Surprisingly, he doesn't become even more enraged. He simply smiles in a chilling way.

"You hate her, don't you?"

"Yes," I hiss.

"Good. That might save you."

KARL

"Do you hear that?" Cheryl looks up.

We can't see much of the sky thanks to the canopy of giant leaves and branches. They also hide whatever is making that grating sound.

"Buzzing. We need to find cover now," Ronan orders.

I look around and see nowhere to go. *Fuck.* "It's too late to hide."

Cheryl understands my meaning, and in an instant, she shifts. I do the same, but instead of feeling better now that I can fight whatever is coming our way, all my senses home in on Manu's scent, which is now amplified to my wolf senses. The instinct to run after her trail becomes overwhelming. I haven't felt this need to protect her in a long time, and I don't know if the reason is that we're in Ellnesari or her life is in danger.

"Fucking Christ," Ronan mutters. "What's that thing?"

A giant monster akin to something straight out of a mad scientist's lab is flying toward us. I can only describe it as a cross between a man and a hornet. Instinctively, I know getting stung by it will be fatal.

"Oh my God. What's between his legs?" Cheryl asks me via our mind link. *"Is he aroused?"*

"That's what you notice first? Not his giant stinger?"

"Shut up, Karl."

Ronan has unsheathed his sword and is ready to cut the monster in half. But a second buzzing comes from behind us.

"Fuck, there are two!" I yell.

"Shift back. You'll have better chances using a blade," Ronan commands.

Hell, he's right. Cheryl returns to her human form, and Ronan tosses one of his spare weapons to her, but my wolf refuses to cooperate.

"Karl, what are you waiting for?" she asks.

Hell, now I can't explain to her. Our mind-to-mind connection only works when we're both in our wolf forms.

"He needs to go after Manu," Ronan replies for me.

She whips her face to him, ignoring the approaching danger. "How do you know?"

His eyes connect with hers. "Because that's what I'd do if I were in his shoes."

The fucking asshole. I can't believe he just confessed that. I'd rip his throat out in any other circumstance.

Cheryl's face contorts in pain. Her eyes fill with tears, and it only makes me hate the bloodsucker more.

She looks at me. "Go, Karl. Go save your mate."

It's impossible to miss the tightness in her voice, but like the badass she is, she squares her shoulders and faces the second aberration with her sword ready.

I spare Ronan another loathing stare before I run after Manu.

Thirty

RONAN

ITALY, 1521

I woke up a few hours before sunset and headed to the feeding room. Significantly fewer vampires were present at that hour, and the new blood volunteers wouldn't arrive until a few hours after sundown. I had to make do with what was left from the night before. That meant feeding on a human who wouldn't ignite anything beyond regular hunger.

These days, not even the most stunning beauty entices me. I can only think about one female, the wolf shifter, who wants nothing to do with me. I even changed my feeding schedule so she wouldn't catch me going in or out of the feeding room.

With my belly full, I head for the training room. Any moment I have free, I spend there. There's no time for rest when the call of battle can happen at a moment's notice.

I hear grunts before I step foot inside. Cheryl is hanging upside down from wooden bars, doing crunches. In that position, her loose tunic has slid to her chin, revealing her stomach's smooth skin and also the bandage she used to secure her breasts.

The desire that had been absent during my feeding makes itself known. My gums ache, and my mouth turns dry. Raw need courses through my veins like liquid fire. I haven't had this visceral reaction to her in a long time, mostly because I've been careful not to stare at her for too long.

I can't let her catch me like this. One glance in my direction and she'll see my exposed fangs and the glow of my red eyes. Taking deep breaths, I curl my hands into fists and look at the floor.

"What are you doing standing there like a statue?" she asks.

Fuck. I should have walked out.

"Nothing," I grit out. "I thought I'd have the room to myself for a few hours."

The soft thud of her feet landing tells me she jumped off the bar. "I can go."

I lift my chin, hoping I no longer look like a deranged vampire on the verge of bloodlust. "You don't need to leave on my account."

She cocks her head to the side. "Are you okay?"

I shift my stance, trying to appear relaxed, something I'm far from. "Yes. I'm fine. Have you gone through your sword exercises already?"

She twists her face into a scowl. "No. You know I dislike blades."

I walk over to the far wall where our training swords are. "The enemy doesn't care about your preferences. They'll cut you in half just the same."

"Can we do something different today?"

Curious, I look over my shoulder. "What do you have in mind?"

"How about we spar without them?"

My eyebrows arch. "You want to train in hand-to-hand combat?"

"I haven't punched anyone in a while." She smiles, and my damn heart lurches forward.

I should say no. Fighting without a weapon means getting

close, and that's a dangerous situation I don't need. But I can't resist the temptation of it.

A chuckle comes out of my mouth despite my turmoil. "And you won't change that tonight."

"What's the matter, Ronan? Are you afraid to lose to a female?"

I grin and then take off my shirt, lobbing it to the side. Cheryl's green eyes widen as they focus on my naked chest and abs. My smile broadens.

"I'm not afraid," I say. "I was just stating a fact."

Slowly, I walk over, trying to contain the satisfaction of picking up the changes in Cheryl's heartbeat and breathing. Her pupils are dilated, and her scent has a new nuance to it. It's more alluring now, seductive, and almost irresistible.

"And you called me cocky when we first met," she mutters.

"Quit stalling."

I begin to circle her like she's prey. Her body tenses as she gets into her fight stance. I could have attacked before she had the chance to prepare, but I don't want to win easily. I'm looking forward to a challenge.

I'm determined to bide my time before I engage, but I should have known Cheryl wouldn't want to go slow. She attacks at the first opportunity, faster than any opponent I've had in the past. I lift my arms to block her punch, leaving my midsection exposed. She delivers a kick to my stomach, making me grunt, then jumps back, grinning like a fiend.

"You were saying?"

I narrow my eyes. "Don't celebrate yet, darling. We're just starting."

I move fast, becoming a blur, to attack from behind, locking my arms around her neck and frame before she can break free. It'd be impossible for her to escape now if my body didn't betray me. This close to her, her scent becomes intoxicating, and it does my head in. My ears can only hear the sound of her blood pumping in her veins. I want to sink my fangs into her milky flesh and drink from her even though I just ate.

Before I can stop myself, I bring my lips to her neck.

She tenses in my arms and whispers, "Ronan, what are you doing?"

"I don't know," I murmur, then lick her neck.

She arches her back, melting into me, but the next thing I know, there's a sharp pain on my nose when the back of her head connects with it hard. I stagger back, releasing her at once.

"Fuck!"

With one of my hands covering my nose, I can't prevent her from tossing me onto the ground and straddling me. She lifts my arms over my head and leans down.

"I win."

My cock strains against my pants, giving me a new kind of ache. Her face is so close to mine, all I have to do is lift my head to capture her mouth.

A throat clearing by the entrance prevents me from making another mistake.

"Am I interrupting?" Lucca asks, smiling from ear to ear.

Cheryl jumps off me and gives me a wide berth. "You just missed me kicking your friend's ass."

I get to my feet and turn my back to them, trying to hide the evidence of my arousal. "I'm surprised to see you here so early, Luc."

"I was sent to find you two. Uncle Raphael has requested your presence."

The mention of the king sobers me up quicker than a dive in a cold lake.

"What does he want with us?" Cheryl asks.

"I don't know," Lucca replies. "He didn't say."

I head over to where my shirt fell and put it on. "We'd better not leave the king waiting, then."

CHERYL

The king summoned us to give us a mission. He wants us to visit a village an hour from the fortress and see if the inhabitants are in need of anything. There are non-blueblood vampires and humans living there, and they all have pledged their alliance to King Raphael.

As I try to pay attention to the landscape, my mind wanders back to what happened in the training room. Ronan licked my neck, and I liked it so much, I might have let things go further. He never did a good job at hiding his attraction to me. In the beginning, I hated his interest, but mainly because I didn't care for any bloodsucker. Now that I know them better and no longer harbor ill intentions toward them, I crave his attention.

Ronan seemed determined to ignore the sexual tension between us until today. I glance at him, so tall and imposing on top of his horse, and feel the twinge of desire returning to my core. I shake my head, trying to dissipate the lustful fog from my brain and, in consequence, my body.

I force my eyes to stay focused on the village that looms closer. I expected a small cluster of huts, not the sprawling houses that spread down the valley.

"Whoa, that's a city, not a village," I say.

"You haven't been to a real city, then. Come on."

He kicks his horse and increases the pace. I do the same, but my horse isn't as fast as his, so I fall behind. He must have noticed it, but he doesn't slow down until he reaches the center of the village. I would have gotten here first if I was in my wolf form, but not all vampires are open to the idea of a wolf roaming around. In fact, I catch some unwelcoming stares aimed at me.

A tall and wiry man walks forward to greet Ronan. They exchange pleasantries, and then Ronan does what he was ordered by the king to do: gather information. I keep quiet and observe. Despite some animosity toward me, everything is calm here, and I begin to relax.

Not a heartbeat later, the hairs on the back of my neck stand on end, and my entire body tenses. Something isn't right. My horse is restless, also sensing a disturbance in the air.

"Ronan—" I start only to be cut off by a scream.

In an instant, the sound of horses galloping toward us mixes with more panicked cries. Pandemonium ensues, and the acrid smell of smoke reaches my nose. I try to control my horse, but I'm not used to riding.

Ronan reaches for my reins, but an arrow cuts through the air and zooms between us, missing his arm by a hair. My horse rears suddenly. I lose my balance and fall off.

'"Cheryl!" Ronan screams, but it's muffled by all the other noises around us.

My survival instincts take over, and my wolf bursts through. I jump out of the way of my horse's hooves and then look for the bastard with the crossbow. I see him perched on top of a cart and take off in his direction.

It's time to kill some vampires.

Thirty-One

MANU

ITALY, 1521

I attack the dummy with such force that not only do I cut *it* in half but also the frame it was hanging from. Sweat dots my forehead, and some droplets roll into my eyes, stinging them. It's only then that I wipe them off.

"Are you imagining that dummy is Uncle, sis?" Lucca asks from his comfortable position leaning against the wall.

"No," I grumble.

"You know he didn't do it to be mean to you."

I whip my face to him. "He sent Karl away on a stupid mission with Derek. Don't tell me he didn't do it on purpose."

Lucca pushes himself off the wall, then walks over, takes my sword from me, and then steps back. Maybe he's afraid I'll cut through him if he opens his mouth to defend Uncle Raphael again. He's right to be careful. I'm beyond angry.

"The wolf is not his guest but a part of his army. If he wishes to remain under the king's protection, he must contribute."

"He's not a soldier! He's my mate!"

Lucca winces at my outburst and then shakes his head. "You

say Karl is your mate as if that's all he is. You seem to have forgotten he was the son of an alpha, destined to rule. He needs a purpose besides warming your bed."

Blush creeps up my cheeks, but not from shame. I couldn't care less if the entire castle knows about my sex life. His comment just reminded me of what I'm not getting at the moment.

"Besides," Lucca continues, "I didn't see him complain about the mission. In fact, he seems pleased to be of service to the crown."

I open and shut my mouth, but I can't argue with that. Karl was happy to go, excited even. Maybe that's also contributing to my foul mood.

I turn around. "Ugh, I hate when you're right."

He places a hand on my shoulder. "He'll be fine and back before you know it."

I shrug his hand off me. "It's easy for you to say that. You've never been in love."

"And I plan to avoid it for as long as I can. Watching you pine for your mate and then having to deal with Ronan's infatuation with Cheryl are enough reasons for me to not want that fate for me."

"Wait. Ronan is in love with Cheryl?" I can't help my surprise. "Are you certain?"

"You haven't noticed?"

I shake my head and then wait for jealousy to pierce my chest. But I feel nothing.

No, that's not true. I do feel something. Happiness for him if she reciprocates his affections. I don't think I would have felt the same before Karl came into my life. How things have changed.

"I suppose I shouldn't be astonished that you didn't know," Lucca continues. "You've had your head in the clouds since Karl entered the scene."

"My head has not been in the clouds," I retort. "You make me sound like I'm a stupid female who only concerns herself with marriage and babies."

Lucca opens his mouth to comment, but Dean comes running into the training room with eyes wide as if he's seen a ghost.

"There's been an attack near our borders," he announces, out of breath.

Tension sweeps over me. We knew Tatiana would eventually strike near our home, but none of Uncle's spies reported any activity that told us when. If Uncle Raphael hadn't been so reluctant to attack first, perhaps this war would be over by now.

"Where?" Lucca asks.

"The village north of here. It's all I know."

I exchange a worried glance with Lucca. "That's where Ronan's party went earlier this evening."

"This can't be a coincidence."

No it can't. This is the second surprise attack by Tatiana's army. It seems we have a spy among us.

My problems disappear in an instant. Lucca and I hurry out of the training room and find a stream of nervous activity in the hallway. Soldiers and guards run to get their weapons and put their armor on. We do the same and then rush out of the building into the courtyard.

A small army has gathered around Uncle Raphael, who is already up on his horse. I don't see our mother anywhere or James and his Red Guard soldiers. They weren't part of Ronan's party, but that doesn't bring me comfort. They could have gone to the village already. It's not in my mother's nature to wait when people need her help.

We breach through the line until we're standing at the front. Uncle acknowledges our arrival with a simple nod and then looks at the crowd.

"As you may have heard, Tatiana's forces launched an attack on the village north of here. Those are civilians who have pledged their alliance to me, the rightful king."

"What happened to the party we sent there earlier?" I ask.

"We do not know. The sentry only said it was a bloodbath. We have no idea how many losses are on our side, only that they were outnumbered."

My stomach bottoms out. I think about Ronan and Cheryl, and worry consumes me. They have to be all right; I don't dare to imagine a different outcome.

"We must make haste," Uncle says.

That's his cue for everyone to get ready. His soldiers quickly find their mounts or get in formation and prepare to march.

Uncle begins to turn his horse around, but Lucca reaches for the reins and stops him. "Where are Mother and the Red Guard?"

"They left earlier to meet with a group of Nightingale representatives."

"So they don't know about the attack in the village?" I ask.

"The High Witch is with them, so I believe it's possible they may know. But they're too far from the village, and I can't hope they'll return before it's too late."

Before we even have a visual of the village, the stench of carnage reaches my nose. Blood spilled mixes with the odor of burned flesh. The massacre isn't over yet. The noise of swords clashing competes with the screams of the desperate.

We increase our pace and quickly reach the edge of the village —or what's left of it. Fire consumes most of the houses, and smoke has taken over the landscape.

"Bastards," Uncle mutters before he lets out a war cry and charges ahead.

I kick my mount, urging it to keep pace with my uncle's horse, but soon I lose sight of him and Lucca in the smog. Adrenaline shoots up my veins, and my fangs drop. When I find the first enemy soldier, he's busy skewering a poor villager. My vision becomes tinted in crimson. I charge, and with one slash of my sword, I detach his head from the rest of his body before he has the chance to glance my way.

More assholes appear from all sides, but they're all weaklings and no match for me. I lose track of how many of the bastards I cut down as I carve a path toward the center of the village, looking for Ronan and Cheryl.

As I get near the inferno, my horse protests, making it difficult to control it.

"Fuck!"

I circle back, not willing to give up the advantage of higher ground. Now and then, I encounter more of Tatiana's sycophants, but their numbers are much less than before. They either fell under the blade of our army or fled like the cowards they are.

The sound of battle begins to quiet down until only the cries of those who survived remain. With my heart stuck in my throat, I head back to the outskirts of the village where we were instructed to regroup. My stomach bottoms out when I count far fewer soldiers gathered there than before, and there's no sign of Lucca, Ronan, Cheryl, or Uncle Raphael.

I see one of my uncle's most seasoned soldiers and make my way to him. I need information. Before I can get to him, a lonely figure comes running toward us. At first I mistake the male for a villager, but once he's near, I recognize Dean. He's covered in soot and blood, and there's a big gash in his armor near the shoulder.

"You need a healer," I tell him.

His eyes are wide and frantic. I'm not sure he recognizes me. I get down from my horse so I can look at him closer. Finally, his gaze loses the unfocused glint. He grabs my arms and shakes me.

"I tried to help him, but there were too many, far too many."

"Help who?"

"Lucca," he whimpers and then releases me to hug his middle. "They came out of nowhere. I couldn't warn him in time."

"Where is he?" I scream.

He points a shaky finger in the direction he came from.

I rush back to my horse and don't wait for anyone to follow me. My heart is racing at the same breakneck speed as my mount. I don't see anything but fallen bodies on my way, and none of them are Lucca. I cross the entire village and am about to make my way back when I smell his blood.

"No."

I kick my horse's flank again, urging it to go up the hill in front of me. Then I see him, lying on the ground in a pool of his own blood. But he's not dead. He's clutching a robed female and feeding from her.

It's then that I notice my mother, standing not far from him and crying.

"Mother!" I call her name as I jump off my horse.

She turns to me, revealing her tear-streaked face. My uncle's towering form joins us from the other side a moment later.

"Natalia, what happene—Lucca, no! You'll kill her." He starts toward my brother, but my mother blocks his way.

"If he doesn't drink it all, he'll die."

Uncle Raphael's eyes widen. "Natalia, are you mad? That's a Nightingale priestess."

Lucca makes a distressed sound, earning our attention. The priestess's body rolls off his, lifeless.

Shit. He did drink her dry.

Mother runs to him and pulls him into her arms. "You're okay, you're okay."

A gust of violent wind erupts around us. It's filled with magic, Nightingale magic. I raise my arms to shield my face from the debris the tornado is sending our way. The pressure builds, sending me to my knees. I cry out as my ears ring from the piercing sound.

"You vile creatures!" a female shrieks.

The wind has slowed a bit, allowing me to look up and see a beautiful Nightingale dressed in a white gossamer gown. She glares at us with her strange, silver eyes.

"Queen Maewe, it was an accident," my uncle says, subdued.

I've never seen him act submissive like that.

"Silence! Your sister knew very well what she was doing when she lured one of my priestesses here."

Mother clutches Lucca tighter against her chest, even though he fights to break from her embrace and meet the Nightingale queen like a grown male.

"He was dying," Mother says.

With a flick of her hand, she sends Lucca flying across the hill. He falls on his side, near me. I see then the gash on his neck that has recently healed thanks to the Nightingale priestess's blood. He was nearly decapitated.

"No!" Uncle Raphael screams.

I turn toward his desperate cry and let out one of my own as Mother's headless body falls to the side.

"You killed her," Lucca cries. "You evil bitch."

He staggers to his feet, but he can barely stand.

"Lucca, don't say another word." Uncle Raphael raises a supplicant hand.

"I said silence!" The queen moves her fingers, and immediately my uncle clutches his neck and tries to draw air in. He can't. She's suffocating him with her powers. He won't die in that manner, but he will suffer.

In a frenzy, Lucca rushes toward the female. But quicker than a snake, she moves and then has him hanging in the air as she squeezes his neck.

"Let him go." I try to get up, but a great force pushes me down and keeps me there, flattened against the earth.

"I ought to kill you for what you've done, but that would be too quick, too easy," she seethes. "I want you to suffer."

He tries to pry her fingers open, but the female looks like she's made of marble.

"Please, let him go," I beg through tears.

"Lucca Della Morte, I hereby curse you to die a slow and

painful death. The blood from mortals will never nourish you completely, and with time, your strength will wane until you're no better than a rat. You'll always crave Nightingale blood for it's the only substance capable of restoring your vigor. But a simple whiff will send you into bloodlust. You won't be able to think, to speak, to do anything besides satiate your hunger. And when you kill your second Nightingale, your soul will be condemned to eternal damnation."

She releases him then as if he were a sack of rotten food.

I still can't move, so when she floats toward me, there's nothing I can do but stare. She grabs my hair and yanks hard, bringing my face up from the ground.

"What shall I do with you?" She peers into my eyes as if she's trying to read my thoughts.

"Manu has done nothing, my queen. Please let her go," Uncle Raphael begs.

She must have released the magic around him when she cursed Lucca.

"You are way too pretty for a savage beast. That doesn't please me. Ah... but you have a mate who is also your familiar. Making you grotesque won't matter to him." Her lips twist into a malicious grin. "I'll take away your looks *and* your love, then."

"No! You can't kill Karl. He's done nothing to you."

"Oh, I'm not killing the wolf, darling. You'll do that on your own. Your curse is to kill what you love the most. A single kiss and it's adieu, little pet. Try to warn him, and he dies."

I feel it in my bones when the curse sets in. It crushes my soul; it makes me want to shrivel and die. But the odious magic from the evil queen doesn't stop. She's doing something to me, yet I don't have the will to care.

"Stop!" Uncle Raphael is suddenly there, holding Queen Maewe's wrist.

Her eyes spark with fury, and I see her turn her magic on him. Before my eyes, his dark hair turns gray. He releases her arm and steps back.

"Are you done?" he asks in a voice that's dangerously low.

Something happened to him. He's no longer trying to appear small to please the bitch queen.

She smirks. "I'm far from done, my dear."

In the blink of an eye, she's gone.

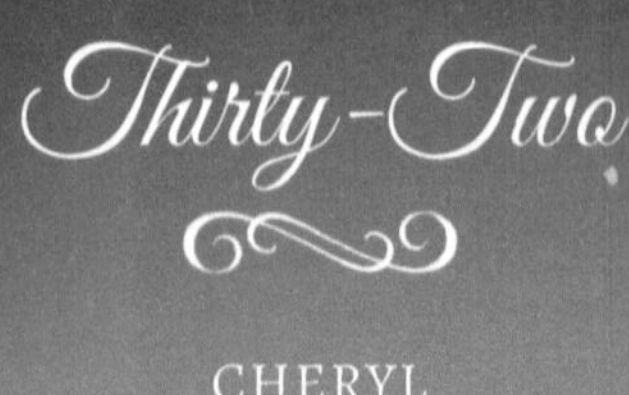

Thirty-Two

CHERYL

ITALY, 1521

No matter how many bloodsuckers I take down, they won't stop coming. It's clear we're outnumbered. The small unit of soldiers stationed at the village isn't enough to stop the onslaught. Ronan and I manage to stick together as we battle. This is the first time we've fought together on the same side, and I couldn't have asked for a better partner. We're so in sync it's almost as if our minds are linked.

Even with the odds stacked against us, I have hope that we can hold off the enemy until reinforcements arrive. But my optimism crumbles like a sandcastle when a foreign power interferes. I sense the wrongness in the air even before Ronan's movements become sluggish, which almost costs him his head.

I realize that magic is being used, *dark* magic, but somehow I'm immune to it. I try to locate the mage responsible in the middle of the chaos. It's easier than I thought; so sure that he had the upper hand, he didn't bother concealing himself. I make a beeline toward him, and when he sees me coming, he tries to hit me with another spell. I jump out of the way, missing being blown to smithereens by a hair, but the impact of the explosion knocks me down, making me dizzy for a moment.

When I get back to my feet, the mage is already on the run. I look over my shoulder, searching for Ronan. He's recovered the ability to move unhindered, but he's now surrounded by three bloodsuckers. I can't leave him behind to chase the mage.

I prepare to jump on the closest vampire to me when I feel a sting in my neck. Before I know what hit me, my body begins to shift back. *No. Wolfsbane.* For all the months I took the poison, I couldn't stop it from causing a reversal of shift. I take solace in the fact that I'm not at the mercy of the drug anymore. I can still move my body and defend myself.

I'm mid-rise when my hair is yanked back and a blade presses against my throat. The stench of death reaches my nose, bringing bile to my mouth.

"My, my, aren't you a pretty thing? I've never had wolf pussy before."

"Boone! Let go of her!" Ronan yells from too far. He's still busy fighting too many bastards.

The vampire behind me laughs. "Ah, you're McLaren's pet. Even better."

I struggle against his hold, which only makes the blade cut my skin. My captor drags me away from Ronan and the thick of the battle. Then he enters a dwelling that's not engulfed in flames and tosses me to the ground, unconcerned that I might try to escape. He thinks I'm useless because of the wolfsbane. I let him believe that as I watch him fiddle with the laces of his pants. I'm shaking with rage, but I must keep it from showing on my face. He needs to believe he's about to rape a defenseless female.

"I should have taken wolf females before. I love seeing the desperation in your eyes when you can't do anything."

Done with his pants, he moves toward me, covering my breasts with his disgusting hands. My stomach twists, and the urge to puke is immense. I must endure it and let him have his fun so I can steal one of the blades from his leg holster, but he's a sadistic bastard and bites my shoulder before I can. It kicks my survival instincts into overdrive, and I show my hand by punching him in the head.

"You fucking bitch! You shouldn't be able to move."

He's on top of me and has the advantage, but I give him hell nonetheless. I claw and slash his cheeks. There's so much fury in me that I barely feel the sting of his blow on my face.

"I'm going to make you pay for this." He holds me by the neck, cutting off my air supply, while he pries my legs open.

Tears sting my eyes as the realization that he'll get what he wants sinks in.

A roar echoes inside the hut, and then the vampire is yanked off me.

Ronan is here. He came for me.

My relief is short lived when I notice one of his arms seems to be broken. Boone is fresh and takes full advantage of that. He charges, quickly pushing Ronan into a corner. I have to help him.

Frantically, I search for something inside the dwelling that I can use as a weapon. The rod of the fire poker catches my eye. I dive for it, but when I turn, I know I won't have time to run back to Boone. Ronan lost his sword and is about to receive the death blow. I throw the poker with all my strength, aiming for the only part of the vampire's body not protected by metal: his neck.

The pointy end finds its mark. Boone releases his sword and clutches his neck, making a gurgling sound. He staggers back and turns. Blood sputters from his mouth, and his round eyes tell me he wasn't expecting this outcome. Unfortunately, the wound isn't fatal. Vampires can only be killed by decapitation, sunlight, and getting their hearts ripped out from their chests.

His condition is precarious though. He can't fight like that. But before Ronan is able to finish him off, the coward runs out of the house.

With a grunt, Ronan falls to his knees, hugging his middle with his good arm. I cross the small space and drop in front of him.

"Are you okay?" I ask as I survey his face. There are a few gashes, but they don't look like they're healing yet.

"I'll live. I'm sorry."

"Why are you sorry?"

"For not getting here sooner. Did he...?"

"No, he didn't."

Relief shines in his eyes, but also guilt.

I touch his face, needing the skin-to-skin connection. "Why aren't your wounds healing yet?"

"Whatever that fucking mage did to me is preventing it."

"What can I do to help?"

He doesn't answer, but the anguish in his eyes tells me all I need to know.

"You need blood," I say.

"Cheryl, I can manage without it. That bastard bit you. You already suffered blood loss. Besides, I know how you fe—"

I cover his mouth with my fingers. "You don't know anything about my feelings, Ronan. Absolutely nothing. And I'm fine. That motherfucker didn't hurt me as much as he thinks he did."

I rub my fingers over his lips, making them part. His eyes change from blue to red in an instant, and my heart beats faster. I move closer and straddle him, careful not to hurt him further. He rests his hand on my thigh, burning my skin. I forgot I was naked until now. But I'm not here to sex him up. He needs to feed, so I pull my hair back and tilt my head to the side, offering my neck.

"Cheryl...," he whispers in a tight voice. "Are you sure?"

"Yes. Take as much as you need."

My body trembles when he brings his lips to my neck. He doesn't bite at first. Instead, he places an open kiss on my throat that sends a zing of pleasure straight down to my core. A gasp escapes my lips as I hold on to his arms and close my eyes.

When the bite comes, there's no pain, only pure ecstasy. Now I understand why so many humans are happy to be food for the vampires. I never knew it could feel this good. Without meaning to, I begin to move my hips, mimicking what I've fantasized about for a while.

Ronan's hand slides off my thigh to cup my sex. I cry out, all sense of reality turning into smoke. He rubs his thumb over my nub, sending my pleasure to new heights. With each sweep of his thumb and each pull of his tongue and mouth, I move closer to the edge. An explosion of stars appears before my eyes, and I become bodiless. I say his name out loud, lost in the sensation.

The pressure on my neck eases off, and then Ronan licks the incisions his fangs made. With my eyes still closed, I rest my cheek against his chest and wait for my heartbeat to return to normal.

"We need to find clothes for you and then head out. The fight isn't over yet," he says.

Guilt pierces my chest. Innocent blood was spilled while I was having an earth-shattering orgasm.

"Right, we need to go." I slide off his lap and get up, not daring to look into his eyes.

His hand finds my shoulder. "Don't feel guilty about what happened. Feeding and sex go hand in hand for vampires."

"Yes, but you forgot one detail." I look at him. "I'm not a vampire."

Thirty-Three

KARL

ITALY, 1521

"She doesn't want to see anyone, Karl. Please be patient," Lucca says as he stands in front of Manu's quarters.

I was away on a mission with Derek Blackwater when Natalia's forces attacked the village. I knew something terrible had happened and insisted on returning to the fortress immediately. I was willing to say fuck the mission and leave the king's spy behind, but Derek agreed to return with me. I couldn't have imagined the tragedy I found upon my arrival.

Natalia Della Morte dead, and Lucca and Manu cursed. Not even the king escaped unscathed from the wrath of the Nightingale queen.

It's been a week since my return, and I have yet to see my mate. My wolf is restless, and my heart yearns to be near her, to offer comfort. Cheryl told me what the queen did to Manu. She washed away all her coloring, turning her hair white and her irises yellow.

"Tell her I don't care about her looks. I love her!" I yell, losing my patience.

Lucca takes my outburst without a flinch or a rise of his own temper.

"She knows you do, Karl. But... she's been through a lot." He pauses and looks away. "We all have."

Sudden guilt makes me ashamed of my behavior. I've been so lost in my own pain that I ignored Lucca's and Manu's loss.

Shaking my head, I step away from him. "I'm sorry. I know it's been difficult for your family. I...." The ache in my chest is so acute, I can barely say the next words. "I'll wait for her to come to me."

"Thank you, Karl. Don't lose faith."

I nod and then stride away before I shift spontaneously and my wolf takes control. I can feel it swirling in my chest, trying to make me turn around and knock that door down. I should allow my savage beast to burst free, but nowhere near the fortress. It's too dangerous for my wolf to be close to Manu and be denied her company.

I could do with fresh air, though, so I head to the nearest exit, which leads me to one of the outside training areas. The sun hasn't set yet, so the place is empty. Or so I thought. A flash of red hair catches my eye. Cheryl is practicing her sword work. Since we moved into the fortress, she's made it no secret that she detests her lessons in sword combat. But King Raphael was adamant that both of us receive the training.

She's completely in the zone and doesn't notice my approach until I make my presence known by clearing my throat. She jumps on the spot, startled.

"What the hell, Karl? You scared me."

"I can't believe you didn't pick up my scent the moment I stepped foot outside."

"I was distracted. Clearly." She lowers her sword and cocks her head to the side. "Another unfruitful attempt to see your mate?"

I sit on the grass and glance at the sky. "Yes. Lucca wouldn't let me in."

"She asked him to stand guard outside her door?" Her voice rises to a pitch.

"No, he followed me."

Cheryl doesn't speak for several beats as she stares into the distance. "I don't understand. Is she depressed because of what happened to her mother?"

"I'm sure she is. But I think there's something more, something Lucca and the king aren't saying."

She glances at me. "Do you think it has to do with her curse?"

"Maybe."

Cheryl drops her sword to the ground and sits next to me. "Whatever it is, Ronan doesn't know about it either."

"And how do you know that?"

Her face becomes pinker. It's been a while since Cheryl stopped staring at Ronan with annoyance. I suspect she might like him as more than just a friend.

"I asked him."

"And do you believe he was truthful?"

She turns to me. "He wouldn't lie to me."

I narrow my eyes to slits. "I see. I didn't realize you've become so close to the vampire. I remember vividly the time when the mere mention of his name would make you see red."

"Many things have changed since then, Karl. I had to eventually expand my circle of friends."

"Hmm."

We remain in silence for a while. Something is consuming Cheryl's thoughts, and I'd bet a limb it has to do with Ronan. But I have my own issues to occupy my mind.

When the sun sets, she jumps to her feet. "I'd better go inside and take a bath. I don't want any of those bloodsuckers saying we're filthy animals."

I wait until she's gone to do what I should have done as soon as I returned from my trip and Manu refused to see me.

I'm going to pay Solomon a visit.

MANU

No sooner does Lucca enter my room than I whirl on him. "What the hell, Lucca?"

"What did I do?"

"You told Karl to have faith. What were you thinking?"

"What did you want me to tell him?" He throws his hands in the air. "He's your mate. You can't keep avoiding him forever."

Tears of frustration and sorrow prick my eyes. I don't want Lucca to see me shed them, so I cover my face and turn around.

"I know, but what choice do I have?" My voice cracks. "If I let him get close to me, he dies."

"You could tell him the truth."

I whirl around, angry now. "I can't! Didn't you hear her? If I tell him, he dies too."

Lucca watches me with his warm brown eyes and patient expression. He was also cursed, but here he is trying to help me, and I'm treating him like he's the enemy.

"She said *you* couldn't tell him, but she never said *I* couldn't."

I shake my head, and the movement makes the tears in my eyes roll down my cheeks. When I think my heart couldn't break more, it shatters into even smaller pieces.

"I can't risk it. She's a conniving bitch, and it's in the Nightingales' nature to be extremely cruel. She would have guessed we'd try that route."

"Is that it, then? You're just going to send the love of your life away forever? Did you forget he's also your familiar?"

I pull my hair back, yanking at the now white strands. "I didn't forget."

Lucca approaches and then pulls me into a hug. "Maybe we can find another Nightingale who can break the curse, Manu."

"It could take centuries, Luc. How do I protect Karl until then?"

"I don't know, sis. I don't know. But we'll figure it out."

First, that hateful female took our mother. Now Karl. Rage surges in the pit of my stomach, coating my sadness with determination and turning my heart to stone.

I turn around in his arms. "I'm going to kill Queen Maewe, Lucca. Even if it takes centuries and it's the last thing I do. I'm going to kill that bitch. That's my vow."

Thirty-Four

MANU

ITALY, 1521

My self-imposed isolation ends when Uncle Raphael summons me. He hasn't visited me the entire time I was locked away in my chambers. He must believe every horrible thing that happened to us was his fault.

I knew my time alone was expiring, but at least now I have a clear purpose to keep me going, even when it feels like I can't. The promise of retribution infuses me with strength. I'm going to end Queen Maewe's reign of terror, no matter the cost.

It's with that sentiment swirling in my chest that I head to Uncle's throne room. I have to be strong, but at the same time, I pray I don't cross paths with Karl. I might collapse like a house made of straw.

The two guards stationed in front of the double doors can't hide their surprise when they see me. I've refused to look at my reflection, but I can guess how grotesque I must appear. The heartless Nightingale queen wouldn't have it any other way.

I lift my chin and pretend I didn't notice their reaction.

"I'm here to see the king," I say loud and clear.

"Of course, Princess," one of the guards says before he opens the doors for me.

So worried about protecting my heart in case I saw Karl, I didn't shield myself from another part of my cruel reality: my uncle sitting alone on the dais, and my mother's empty throne. For a moment, I can't draw air into my lungs.

My ears ring as I force one foot in front of the other until I'm standing in front of the king. His hair and beard have turned gray, but his eyes are still the same warm brown as before.

He can't hide the pain upon seeing my new appearance, but unlike his guards, he manages to conceal it faster.

I curtsy, bowing my head, and then say, "You wanted to see me, my king?"

"Manu... I...." He clenches his jaw and then stands.

Frozen like a statue, I watch him walk over. When he pulls me into his arms and hugs me, I don't react right away.

"I'm so sorry, child." His voice cracks, and that's my undoing.

I hug him back, burying my face against his chest. For the first time since I returned from the battle in the village, I allow myself to cry for Mom.

"She's going to pay, Uncle," I say. "I'll make her pay, even if it's the last thing I do in my life."

Holding my arms, he pushes me back. "Don't, Manu. Queen Maewe is my problem. I'll deal with her."

"You have no right to tell me I can't seek retribution after what she took from me, from us!"

"I have every right. I'm still your king." His eyes flash crimson.

Tears of anger roll down my cheeks now. I step away from him and hastily wipe them off.

The doors to the chamber open with a bang, and the world seems to go off-kilter. My body is coiled tight as I pivot slowly to look at the newcomer, though I didn't need to see him to know Karl was the one who burst through.

"Manu...." He takes a step forward but stops when I take one back.

Unlike everyone else, he doesn't react to my new coloring. His eyes still regard me with utter devotion and unconditional love. The pull from the mating bond is stronger than ever, and to stay in place and not run to his arms is the hardest thing I've ever had to do.

I shake my head, fighting to keep the tears at bay. "Don't come any closer."

He doesn't heed my words and walks over. "Don't ask me for the impossible."

A whimper escapes my lips. So much for my resolution to remain stoic. I can't when he's looking at me like that.

Uncle Raphael steps in front of me, acting as a shield. "Listen to my niece, Karl."

"I don't understand. Why can't I hold my mate? What happened on that battlefield?"

"You need to leave, Karl," he says.

"No! I won't go without speaking to Manu first. I've been patient. I've waited a fucking week!"

"You dare challenge my orders, boy? I am the king!" Uncle roars. He shoves Karl so hard, he flies back until he hits the far wall.

"Karl!" I walk around Uncle Raphael, but he grabs my arm, stopping me.

"Manu, no."

I struggle against his hold, even though I know why I can't go to Karl. But seeing him hurt triggered the urge to protect my mate.

Karl staggers back to his feet with eyes that are glowing wolfish yellow.

Hell, things are getting out of control fast.

"Guards! Take him," my uncle commands.

Karl snarls at the guards, revealing his fangs. He's going to shift any moment now, and then bloodshed will ensue.

Lucca comes running, followed by the High Witch. Lucca

takes a step forward to help the guards, but Karl sprints forward in his wolf form and pushes my brother to the floor.

The guards unsheathe their swords but wait for my uncle's command before they attack.

"Don't hurt him, please," I beg them.

"Daveena," my uncle says, and it's enough for the High Witch to know what to do.

She raises her hand and recites a spell. Magic spreads in the room like a soft summer breeze. My body relaxes and my head becomes fuzzy. Karl stops growling and then drops to the floor with a whimper.

His eyes meet mine across the room right before he shifts back into his human form. Through the mating bond, I feel everything he does: sadness, confusion, and a deep sense of betrayal. But I also feel his determination to find out the truth, and I can't allow that to happen. I must protect him at all costs, even if that means losing him forever.

Hiding from him won't work, and going away won't either. He'll follow me. The only way I can save him is to make him hate me. I need to crush his soul.

CHERYL

Following the aftermath of the massacre in the village, I kept my distance from Ronan, save for asking him if he knew anything about Manu's and Lucca's curses. What happened in that dwelling, him feeding from me and touching me in places no other male had before, did my head in. I don't know what to think or if I can trust my feelings.

In the last year, I've come to enjoy his company and admire him as a person, but he's still a vampire, and even though I've asked King Raphael if a wolf shifter could be turned, there's still an inbred reluctance to accept Ronan as more than a friend.

Today, I've decided it's high time to have an honest conversation with him. I don't want to walk on my tiptoes when I'm around him or keep pretending he doesn't send a thrill down my spine every time he gives me one of his smoldering glances.

I find him in the courtyard outside, punching a bag filled with grain. I don't say anything, just stand there and watch him practice. Even when I was riding the hate-all-bloodsuckers bandwagon, I couldn't turn a blind eye to the way Ronan is built. I've never seen a more beautiful male. Maybe that contributed to my animosity toward him. The enemy shouldn't look the way he does.

He's so damn tall and muscular, yet he moves as if he's floating on air, limber and agile. The ferocity he displays as he pounds the bag makes me guess he's picturing his most hateful adversary. With a powerful punch, he rips the sack open and then stares at the damage while breathing hard.

"Impressive," I say.

He looks over his shoulder and doesn't say a word for a couple of beats. His eyes are enigmatic, but they beguile me just the same. I walk over, feeling nervous all of a sudden.

"I'll get another sack for you," he says.

"I didn't come here to practice."

He wipes the sweat off his forehead as he turns toward me. My heart is running at breakneck speed, and now that I'm here alone with him, I don't know what I want to say.

He raises an eyebrow. "Does that mean you were looking for me?"

"Yes. I...." I pause to take a deep breath. "I want to talk about what happened last week."

"You're nervous. You don't need to be around me, Cheryl."

"I disagree. I don't like how I feel when I'm in your presence."

His eyebrows furrow. "I don't know how to respond to that."

"I've always been sure of who I was and what I wanted, but when I'm with you, all my convictions evaporate into thin air."

"You're not alone in that regard."

I cock my head to the side. "Is it my blood that you crave?"

He steps forward, invading my personal space. "No."

I have to crane my neck to look into his eyes. "My body, then."

With a gentleness that almost feels impossible coming from such a powerful warrior, he caresses my cheek, sending a zing of pleasure down my back.

"I want everything from you."

His lips find mine, and there's nothing gentle about his kiss. It's savage, controlling, and demanding. I rise on my tiptoes, throwing my arms around his neck to bring him closer to me. It doesn't matter what he is or what I am —this feels right.

All my reservations and my fears disappear as I get lost in him. He wraps his arms around me, and now there's no space left between our bodies. Even with my eyes closed, my world explodes in color. For the first time, there isn't a blanket of doom pressing down on me. Ronan makes me feel alive.

With a grunt, he pulls back, capturing my face between his calloused hands to keep me from following.

"God, I dreamed of doing this for so long," he murmurs.

"Tell me how long."

"Since you moved here."

"But I hated you then."

He shrugs. "The heart wants what the heart wants."

A commotion inside the fortress catches our attention. There are shouts, and then I hear Lucca's voice telling guards to secure the wolf.

Wolf? Could a rogue member of my former pack have made their way here?

Ronan and I jump apart and run to investigate. Inside the fortress, I see one of the guards carrying Karl, who is unconscious.

"What happened to my brother?" I rush after him, but Lucca blocks my way.

"He's fine, Cheryl."

"Let me through, Lucca."

He holds my arms. "I can't. Karl challenged the king. The guards have been ordered to lock him away."

"What? Is your uncle fucking mad?"

I see remorse in Lucca's eyes, but I don't care. I try to break free from his hold, and when I can't, I sense the shift happening.

Ronan pulls me away from Lucca and turns me around. "Calm down, Cheryl. We'll get to the bottom of this. Attacking Lucca won't help you."

I shove him off me. Of course he'd defend one of his own.

"I bet this has to do with his damn sister," I say.

She appears in the hallway then, looking more like a ghost than a vampire. There are tear streaks on her face, but other than that, she seems unbothered about Karl's fate.

I step toward her. "What have you done to my brother?"

She levels me with a cold stare. "I don't owe you any explanation. I'm a princess, and you're nothing but a mutt."

I launch at her in an explosion of fur and teeth. I've never shifted this fast in my life. She barely has time to lift her arms and protect her precious neck as we fall together. My vision is tinged in red, and the fury of my wolf is all I know.

Before I can bite her arm off, I'm yanked away and thrown against a wall. A whimper leaves my mouth as white-hot pain shoots up my back. The blow made me dizzy momentarily, but I still know who came to defend the bitch princess.

Ronan.

I hear the sound of swords being drawn, but I don't get back on my paws to defend myself. I stare at him and let that image seep into my brain. His eyes aren't wide with surprise. They're narrowed and hard. That's not the stare of a lover. That's the stare of the enemy.

Thirty-Five

MANU

ITALY, 1521

The healer has just finished bandaging my arm when Daveena, the High Witch, enters my chambers. With a single glance, she sends the female away. Only when the door closes does she walk over to my seat by the fire.

"How are you feeling?" she asks.

"If you're inquiring about my wound, it's minimal. If you're asking in general... not so great."

"I'll make it my mission to find a cure for your curse. And the mission of my descendants."

"Empty promises. What hope can a witch have of breaking a Nightingale spell?"

Her spine goes rigid. "Don't underestimate the power that courses through my veins, Princess."

I shake my head. "I didn't ask you to come see me in the hopes of a miracle. What I want from you is more attainable."

"What do you need? If it's within my power, I will gladly oblige."

I look her dead in the eye. "I want you to give Karl and Cheryl false memories."

Daveena frowns. "Meddling with the minds of others is against the covenant. Surely you know that."

"But can you do it?"

"It's not a question of whether I can but if I should."

"You know about my curse. If Karl learns about it, he dies. If he believes there's still hope for us and I succumb to the mating bond, he dies."

"Send him away, then. Banish him."

"I can't!" I shout, making Daveena wince.

Shaking my head, I continue. "It's not that simple. He needs to hate me. He needs to loathe me so much that the mere sight of me will make him sick."

"That's beyond cruel, Princess."

I pinch the bridge of my nose. "He'll survive."

"I meant cruel to you."

Tears prick my eyes. I turn my gaze to the fire, hoping the heat will dry them before they fall.

"I don't have a choice."

"I can't make him fall out of love with you. The power of the mating bond is too strong. It can't be severed, especially now that it's been strengthened by the familiar bond."

I didn't even consider that as a possible solution to my problem because I'm selfish and I don't want him to stop loving me.

No, you just want him to pine for you from afar, Manu.

"That wasn't what I had in mind. I want you to make Karl and Cheryl believe I betrayed him with another."

Daveena doesn't speak, so I glance at her again. As I suspected, she's glowering at me.

"You don't need me for that. Go lie with one of your many admirers."

Like I have any admirers left looking the way I do now.

"I don't want to sleep with anyone," I grit out. "I just want Karl to believe I did."

"Let's say I agree to help you. What will you give me in return?"

I watch her through narrowed eyes. "You're the High Witch. You're bound to the king."

"Yes, the king, not you. I risk losing my position in the coven, ruining my reputation."

"Very well. Name your price."

"I want your mother's jewelry."

Her request sends a swirl of fury up to my throat. I don't care for jewels or gold, but those items have personal value to me, and they can't be replaced.

"To what end?"

"It doesn't concern you."

I grind my teeth and bite my tongue. The High Witch is the only person with access to the magic I need for the spell.

"If it's coin you need, I can get you plenty."

"I don't need coin, Princess. You asked me what my price was, and I gave it to you. Take it or leave it."

I curl my hands into fists, unsurprised when my sharp nails pierce my skin.

"Can you also make Lucca and Ronan forget Karl is my mate?"

Her eyebrows arch. "Why would you want that?"

I close my eyes for a second and take a deep breath. "Because I can't bear anyone close to me bringing that up."

She shakes her head. "I'm sorry, but that I cannot do. Altering the memories of your brother would be treason."

My heart becomes tighter.

"Your uncle has the power to do it, though," she continues. "He could compel Lucca and Ronan to forget that detail."

"That would also mean he could give Karl and Cheryl false memories, and then, I wouldn't need your services after all."

Her face becomes paler, and her eyes grow wider as she realizes her mistake.

"I fear such a spell is beyond the king's power. You need me for that, Princess."

From being reluctant to accept my offer to eager to be of service. I'd better keep an eye on her. For now, I have to play nice.

"Very well. You have a deal," I say. "When can it be done?"

Her eyes shine with glee, but she forces a cool mask on her face before she replies, "The spell will only work if the seed of doubt already exists in their minds."

My stomach tightens. There's only one person who fits that prerequisite. I press my eyes closed once more, wrestling with the turmoil in my chest. To ask Daveena to use Ronan in the spell means destroying more lives, not just Karl's and mine. But I can't think of anything else save for cheating on Karl for real.

"Ronan McLaren. He's the one you need to use."

To be continued in FERAL BOND

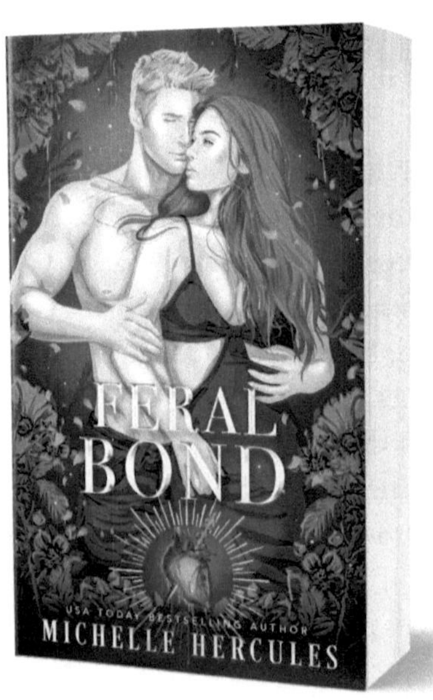

About the Author

USA Today Bestselling Author Michelle Hercules always knew creative arts were her calling but not in a million years did she think she would become an author. With a background in fashion design she thought she would follow that path. But one day, out of the blue, she had an idea for a book. One page turned into ten pages, ten pages turned into a hundred, and before she knew it, her first novel, The Prophecy of Arcadia, was born.

Michelle Hercules resides in Florida with her husband and daughter. She is currently working on the *Blueblood Vampires* series and the *Filthy Gods* series.

Sign-up for Michelle Hercules' Newsletter:

Join Michelle Hercules' Readers Group:
https://www.facebook.com/groups/mhsoars

Connect with Michelle Hercules:
www.michellehercules.com
books@mhsoars.com

facebook.com/michelleherculesauthor
instagram.com/michelleherculesauthor
amazon.com/Michelle-Hercules/e/B075652M8M
bookbub.com/authors/michelle-hercules
tiktok.com/@michelleherculesauthor?